THE BOOK OF LEGENDS

SHORT LEGENDARY STORIES

ANSHOO MITTAL

ISBN 979-8-89906-941-3

Contents

Part II: Cosmic & Celestial Tales

Part III: Guardians, Gods & Mythical Beasts

Part IV: Legends of the Mind & Spirit

Acknowledgments

To the stories that found me before I found the words.

To the ones that whispered in dreams, on long walks, or when I should've been sleeping.

To the people who still believe in things unseen.

And to the ones who don't—maybe this book will change that.

To my WW—for grounding the chaos and standing beside every wild idea.

And to **Dhir**—you've already got the spark.

I just hope the world's ready for what you're going to light up.

Earthbound Legends

*

The Legacy of the Seas

The Legacy of the Seas was the epitome of luxury and grandeur, a 30-story cruise ship that traversed the oceans like a floating palace. With state-of-the-art amenities and unparalleled comforts for its guests, it was renowned as the ultimate dream destination for travelers seeking an unforgettable experience.

Among the ship's most extraordinary features was a small but exquisite 5-acre forest, lovingly tended by skilled horticulturists. This forest was a sanctuary of lush greenery, filled with rare and exotic plants from all corners of the world. It was a tranquil oasis where guests could escape the bustle of the ship and immerse themselves in the beauty of nature.

On a seemingly ordinary day, as the Legacy of the Seas cruised through the Arabian Sea, an unforeseen disaster struck. A violent storm brewed on the horizon, its dark clouds and fierce winds heralding its arrival. The crew, well-trained in handling adverse conditions, braced themselves for the tempest, reassured by the ship's advanced technology and sturdy design.

But the storm proved to be unlike any they had encountered before. With a ferocity that was unprecedented, it lashed against the mighty vessel, causing it to shudder and groan. The waves crashed with such force that they threatened to breach the hull.

The Legacy of the Seas fought valiantly, but it was no match for the relentless onslaught of nature's fury. The ship's systems began to falter, and despite the crew's best efforts, the water breached the lower decks. Panic spread among the passengers as they realized the gravity of the situation.

Amidst the chaos, the ship's captain, Captain Gregory, took charge, displaying remarkable calm and courage. He ordered the evacuation procedures to be initiated, prioritizing the safety of the passengers and crew above all else.

As the lifeboats were lowered into the churning sea, the Legacy of the Seas listed to one side, its fate uncertain. The forest, once a serene sanctuary, was now awash with seawater, its delicate ecosystem threatened by the rising tides.

Captain Gregory stayed on the bridge, coordinating the evacuation and ensuring every last person was safely accounted for. The crew worked tirelessly, displaying remarkable unity and courage, even in the face of impending disaster.

As the last lifeboat departed, Captain Gregory prepared to leave the ship, ensuring he was the last to go. He looked back at the magnificent vessel, now tilting precariously, and felt a pang of sorrow for the Legacy of the Seas.

In those final moments, a sense of solemnity and respect washed over him. The ship had been more than just a vessel; it had been a symbol of dreams realized, adventures shared, and memories made. It had touched the lives of countless passengers, leaving behind a legacy that would endure in their hearts.

With a heavy heart, Captain Gregory stepped onto the last lifeboat, and as the Legacy of the Seas sank beneath the waves, he could only hope that the memories and experiences shared aboard her would forever be cherished.

In the aftermath of the tragedy, the world mourned the loss of the legendary cruise ship. The 5-acre forest, now submerged in the Arabian Sea, became a bittersweet reminder of the Legacy of the Seas and the grandeur it once embodied.

Yet, the story of the ship's legacy lived on. It became a tale of resilience, unity, and the enduring spirit of the human heart. And though the physical vessel may have sunk to the depths, the memories of the journey aboard the Legacy of the Seas would forever sail on in the hearts of those who had been a part of its storied voyage.

The Devil's Playground

In the mystical realm of Cortamalties, where ancient forests merged with snow-capped mountains and cascading waterfalls, there existed a place shrouded in darkness and mystery—the Devil's Playground. This ominous land was said to be cursed, a realm where the malevolent spirits roamed freely, and where the souls of the wicked were condemned to wander for eternity.

Legend had it that centuries ago, a powerful sorcerer named Malachai sought to harness dark magic to attain unmatched power. His insatiable hunger for supremacy led him to delve into forbidden incantations and make deals with sinister entities. In his pursuit of dark knowledge, he inadvertently unleashed a curse upon a secluded valley, transforming it into the dreaded Devil's Playground.

As the years passed, the cursed land became a place of fear and superstition. Tales of eerie sightings, unsettling whispers, and malevolent apparitions filled the hearts of the people of Cortamalties. None dared to venture into the Devil's Playground, fearing they might never return.

But amidst the shadows and fear, a brave and adventurous soul named Elara emerged. She was known for her courage and determination, and she couldn't resist the allure of the unknown. Elara had grown up listening to the legends of the Devil's Playground, and her curiosity burned brighter than any fear.

With her loyal companion, a wise old owl named Orion, perched on her shoulder, Elara set out on a treacherous journey to the cursed land. As she entered the valley, the air grew cold and heavy, and an eerie silence settled around her.

Elara's heart pounded, but she pressed on, guided by a mysterious pull that seemed to draw her deeper into the Devil's Playground. The landscape grew more foreboding with each step, and shadows danced on the periphery of her vision.

As night descended upon the cursed land, Elara heard haunting melodies carried by the wind. Mesmerized, she followed the ethereal music until it led her to an ancient stone monument—the remains of an altar where Malachai had conducted his dark rituals.

Drawn by an unseen force, Elara touched the stone, and a vision of the past unfolded before her eyes. She witnessed the sorcerer Malachai, consumed by greed and thirst for power, unleashing the curse upon the valley, unaware of the horrors it would unleash.

But Elara also saw glimpses of the innocent souls caught in the curse's grasp—children, families, and kind-hearted villagers whose lives were forever altered by the malevolence of dark magic.

Moved by the tragedy she witnessed, Elara resolved to break the curse and free the souls trapped within the Devil's Playground. She knew that it wouldn't be an easy task, but she believed that goodness and light could prevail even in the darkest of places.

With the guidance of Orion and her unwavering determination, Elara embarked on a quest to unravel the mysteries of the curse and find a way to reverse its effects. She sought out ancient tomes, delved into forgotten rituals, and consulted with wise mystics from distant lands.

As the days turned into weeks, and the weeks into months, Elara's efforts bore fruit. She discovered the key to breaking the curse—an ancient ritual that required the embodiment of pure and selfless love.

With her heart full of compassion for the souls trapped within the Devil's Playground, Elara performed the ritual at the very heart of the cursed land. As she chanted the incantations and infused the land with her love, a radiant light spread across the valley, banishing the darkness and freeing the tormented souls.

The curse was broken, and the Devil's Playground was no more. In its place stood a beautiful, serene valley, with vibrant flowers and a gentle breeze that seemed to whisper tales of redemption and hope.

Elara's bravery and selfless love had not only freed the souls but also cleansed the land of its malevolence. The people of Cortamalties celebrated her as a hero, and her name became synonymous with courage and compassion.

And so, the legend of Elara and the Devil's Playground lived on, reminding all who heard it that even in the darkest of places, love and courage could triumph, and that true heroes were those who dared to face their fears and bring light to the shadows.

The Tale of the Sphnex

In a forgotten land where myths and legends intertwined, there stood an ancient marvel—the Sphnex, a colossal statue that was the fusion of two magnificent creatures, the Sphinx and the Phoenix.

The tale of the Sphnex was whispered among the locals, passed down through generations. According to the legend, long ago, an enigmatic sculptor named Darius roamed the land, seeking inspiration from the natural world. He was captivated by the grace and majesty of the Sphinx, with its lion's body and human face, as well as the Phoenix, with its resplendent wings and ability to be reborn from its own ashes.

Filled with a vision that transcended reality, Darius dedicated himself to creating a monument that would embody the wisdom, strength, and eternal spirit of both creatures. For years, he toiled tirelessly, pouring his heart and soul into every chisel stroke and sculpting detail.

At last, the day came when the Sphnex was unveiled to the world. It stood tall and proud, a masterful amalgamation of stone and magic. The lion's body of the Sphinx merged seamlessly with the outstretched wings of the Phoenix, while the human face gazed into the distance with an enigmatic smile, as if holding the secrets of the universe.

The Sphnex soon became a symbol of hope, unity, and wisdom for the people of the land. It was said that those who gazed upon the statue felt a profound sense of awe and enlightenment, as if touched by the spirits of both the Sphinx and the Phoenix.

As time passed, the Sphnex became a sanctuary for seekers of truth and enlightenment. People from all walks of life traveled from far and wide, drawn by the aura of mystique that surrounded the statue. They sought its wisdom, meditated at its feet, and offered prayers for a brighter future.

But, like all legends, a dark cloud loomed on the horizon. An envious sorcerer named Malachi, driven by greed and a desire for power, coveted the Sphnex's mystical energy. He believed that by harnessing the statue's magic, he could bend reality to his will and become all-powerful.

In the dead of night, Malachi crept into the sacred temple that housed the Sphnex. With wicked intent, he unleashed dark spells, hoping to siphon the statue's energy for himself. But the Sphnex was more than just stone and magic; it was imbued with the essence of the Sphinx and the Phoenix— creatures of wisdom and rebirth.

As Malachi's wicked incantations echoed through the temple, the Sphnex came alive with a radiant glow. The statue's eyes glowed with a fiery intensity, and its wings spread wide, casting a brilliant light that pushed back the darkness. The combined spirit of the Sphinx and the Phoenix rose up against the malevolent sorcerer, protecting the sacred monument and driving him away.

The legend of the Sphnex endured through the ages, a tale of wisdom, strength, and the eternal spirit of the Sphinx and the Phoenix. To this day, the statue stands tall, a testament to the power of unity and the triumph of goodness over darkness.

Travelers and seekers still visit the land, drawn by the allure of the Sphnex's enigmatic smile and the magic that lingers in its presence. And amidst the whispers of the wind and the rays of the rising sun, the legend of the Sphnex lives on, reminding all who hear it that there is power in embracing both wisdom and rebirth, and that unity can overcome even the darkest of forces.

The Legend of the Baby Sitters from Mars

In the distant corners of the cosmos, far beyond the reaches of Earth, there existed a vibrant planet known as Mars. On this crimson world, an extraordinary legend was whispered among the stars—the legend of the Baby Sitters from Mars.

Long ago, in the vast Martian metropolis of Cydonia, there thrived a community of kind and compassionate Martians. They were a unique species with large, sparkling eyes, adorned in colorful, flowing garments. Their most remarkable trait was their ability to communicate through a special telepathic connection, making them a close-knit and empathetic society.

But there was something particularly special about certain Martians who were born under a rare celestial alignment. They were believed to possess extraordinary skills in caring for and nurturing young creatures of all species. These gifted individuals were called the Baby Sitters from Mars.

As the legend goes, whenever an endangered or orphaned creature was found on Mars, the Baby Sitters would sense it through their telepathic connection with nature. With hearts full of love and dedication, they would set out on a quest to find and care for these young beings.

Among the most renowned of the Baby Sitters was a young Martian named Lila. With her emerald-green eyes and an aura of kindness, she was beloved by all who knew her. Lila's adventures took her across the Martian deserts, soaring through the crimson skies, and into the depths of ancient caverns, where she would find and nurture creatures in need.

One day, news of a rare and mysterious creature reached Cydonia—the Stellar Phoenix, a mythical bird said to possess the power to heal and bring prosperity. But its magical feathers had been scattered across Mars, making it vulnerable to those who sought its powers for nefarious purposes.

Determined to protect the Stellar Phoenix, Lila embarked on a daring quest to find and safeguard its feathers. Along her journey, she was joined by other Baby Sitters from Mars, each with their own unique gifts and talents.

They faced challenges and dangers at every turn, as dark forces sought to capture the Stellar Phoenix for their own gain. But the Baby Sitters' bond of friendship, their unwavering courage, and their deep connection with the creatures of Mars guided them through even the most treacherous trials.

Together, they collected the Stellar Phoenix's feathers, learning the true power of empathy, trust, and unity in the process. With each feather restored to its rightful place, the Stellar Phoenix regained its strength, illuminating the Martian skies with its brilliant radiance.

Word of the Baby Sitters' heroic efforts spread across Mars, and they became revered as legendary protectors of the planet's creatures. They continued to dedicate their lives to caring for and nurturing young beings, from the smallest of insects to the mightiest of mythical creatures.

As the years passed, the legend of the Baby Sitters from Mars grew beyond the borders of their crimson world. Their compassion, wisdom, and telepathic connection inspired tales among the stars, and they became symbols of hope, unity, and kindness in the vast expanse of the cosmos.

To this day, the legend of the Baby Sitters from Mars lives on, reminding all who hear it of the importance of caring for one another and the creatures that share our world. And though they may be far away among the stars, their spirit of love and protection continues to shine brightly, a beacon of hope in the universe.

Candy Land Walk

Morgan was known for her adventurous spirit, but she never could have imagined the sweet journey that awaited her. One bright and sunny day, as she was hiking through a picturesque meadow, she noticed a peculiar sight in the distance—a swirling vortex of colorful mist that seemed to lead to a different world altogether.

Curiosity got the better of her, and without a second thought, Morgan stepped into the vortex. To her amazement, she found herself in a land beyond her wildest dreams—Candy Land.

Everywhere she looked, there were candy trees, edible flowers, and rivers flowing with melted chocolate. Gummy bears, licorice vines, and marshmallow clouds filled the sky, creating a landscape that looked like it was lifted straight from a child's imagination.

As she explored this enchanting realm, Morgan couldn't believe her luck. She was surrounded by candy of all shapes, colors, and flavors. The air was filled with the tantalizing aroma of cotton candy and freshly baked cookies.

But as she wandered deeper into the candy-filled land, Morgan realized that this world wasn't just about indulging in sweet treats. The inhabitants of Candy Land were friendly and welcoming, and they lived in harmony with the land they called home.

She met the Lollipop Guardians, who were responsible for maintaining the candy trees and ensuring the sweet ecosystem thrived. They explained that while Candy Land was a delightful place, they took care to use the candy responsibly, ensuring that it did not become a wasteful indulgence.

Morgan also encountered the Chocolate Riverkeepers, who were committed to keeping the rivers clean and the chocolate flowing in balance. They explained that even in a land of endless sweetness, moderation and conservation were essential.

As she continued her journey, Morgan learned about the importance of balance and harmony in Candy Land. The inhabitants taught her that while indulging in the candy was part of the joy, it was equally important to appreciate the beauty and wonder of this unique world.

One day, as Morgan was exploring the Candy Land forests, she accidentally stumbled upon a hidden candy cave. Inside, she found a magical candy fountain, said to grant a wish to anyone who tossed a special candy coin into it.

Morgan thought carefully about her wish. Instead of asking for unlimited candy or personal gain, she wished for the well-being of Candy Land and its inhabitants. She hoped that the land's sweetness and magic would endure for generations to come, while also being cherished responsibly.

As she tossed the candy coin into the fountain, a brilliant glow enveloped her. Her wish had been granted, and she felt a deep sense of fulfillment knowing that she had contributed positively to this extraordinary world.

When the time came for Morgan to return to her own world, she bid farewell to her newfound friends with a promise to cherish the memories and lessons she had learned in Candy Land.

As she stepped back through the swirling vortex, Morgan's heart was filled with gratitude for the once-in-a-lifetime adventure she had experienced. She knew that she would forever carry the magic and sweetness of Candy Land in her heart, cherishing the memories of a journey through a world of candy and edibles that taught her the true meaning of balance, moderation, and the joy of discovery.

Morgan's Walk Through the Black Wood's

Morgan was an adventurous soul, always seeking to explore the uncharted and mysterious corners of the world. One fateful day, she heard whispers of a place that sent shivers down the spines of even the bravest souls—the Black Woods. Legend had it that the forest was cursed, haunted by malevolent spirits and shadows that roamed its depths. But tales of this cursed place only fueled Morgan's curiosity, and she knew she had to experience it for herself.

Gathering her hiking gear and armed with a determined spirit, Morgan set out on her legendary hike through the Black Woods. The moment she stepped into the forest, an eerie silence enveloped her, broken only by the faint rustling of leaves and the distant hooting of an owl. The air was heavy with an unsettling energy, but Morgan pressed on, her heart beating with a mixture of fear and excitement.

As she ventured deeper, the trees seemed to close in on her, their branches forming an impenetrable canopy that blocked out the sunlight. Morgan relied on her instincts and a well-drawn map to navigate through the twisted paths, each step taking her further into the unknown.

Strange occurrences began to unfold around her. Shadows danced in the corner of her vision, and eerie whispers seemed to float on the breeze. Yet, Morgan pressed on, undeterred. She believed that beneath the veil of darkness and fear, there might be untold wonders waiting to be discovered.

As the day waned, the forest took on an even more ominous air. A ghostly mist crept along the forest floor, and strange, glowing orbs appeared in the distance, like the eyes of unseen creatures watching her every move. But Morgan's resolve was unyielding, and she pushed forward.

Just as night fell, a faint glimmer of light appeared amidst the darkness. Drawn by the mysterious glow, Morgan followed it deeper into the heart of the Black Woods. To her astonishment, she stumbled upon an ancient stone circle, adorned with mystical symbols and ancient runes. The glow emanated from the center of the circle, where an otherworldly stone stood tall and proud.

Captivated by the sight, Morgan approached the stone, and an overwhelming sense of awe washed over her. The stone seemed to pulse with a strange energy, and as she reached out to touch it, she felt a surge of power surge through her veins.

In that moment, Morgan understood that the legends about the Black Woods were not entirely true. Yes, there were dark and eerie elements, but there was also a hidden beauty and ancient magic waiting to be embraced. The forest held secrets of the past, and Morgan had stumbled upon a place that bridged the gap between the mortal world and the realm of the supernatural.

With newfound wisdom and a heart filled with wonder, Morgan continued her hike through the Black Woods. As the first rays of dawn broke through the trees, she emerged from the forest, forever changed by her legendary journey. She carried with her the knowledge that sometimes, the most extraordinary discoveries lay in the most unexpected and fearsome of places.

From that day forward, Morgan's legendary hike through the Black Woods became a tale that captured the imagination of adventurers and dreamers alike. Her story inspired countless others to face their fears and embrace the mysteries that awaited them in the unknown, for the world is full of wonders and magic, waiting to be explored by those with the courage to seek them out.

The Legend of the Frog Emperor

In a lush and mystical land called Frognar, a legendary tale was whispered among the marshes and ponds—the legend of the Frog Emperor and his formidable Frog Army.

Centuries ago, when Frognar was under constant threat from malicious creatures and power-hungry foes, a wise and noble frog named Aelius rose to power. With his keen intellect and a heart full of compassion for his fellow frogs, Aelius united the scattered frog tribes under his rule, becoming the first Frog Emperor.

Aelius was no ordinary frog; he possessed an extraordinary gift bestowed upon him by the ancient spirits of the marshes. He could communicate with all creatures of the land, both big and small, and he used this gift to forge alliances with the animals of Frognar. Birds would scout from the skies, dragonflies would bring news of distant lands, and turtles would serve as wise advisors.

But it was with his fellow frogs that Aelius formed his most extraordinary bond. Under his leadership, the Frog Army was born—a legion of skilled and courageous frogs, each devoted to protecting their homeland and ensuring peace and harmony reigned in Frognar.

Aelius believed in strength through unity, and he instilled this belief in every member of the Frog Army. Together, they trained relentlessly, honing their agility and mastering the art of camouflage to blend seamlessly into the lush surroundings. They would patrol the marshes and ponds, keeping a vigilant watch for any signs of danger.

One day, a formidable threat emerged from the dark corners of Frognar—an army of voracious serpents led by a malevolent serpent lord named Viperox. This cunning and ruthless creature sought to claim Frognar as his own, lured by the abundance of food that the land provided.

Viperox's army slithered forward, leaving a trail of fear and destruction in their wake. As the serpents encroached on the peaceful habitats of Frognar's inhabitants, panic spread among the creatures of the marshes.

But the Frog Emperor and his Frog Army stood steadfast. Aelius knew that their only chance of victory was to use their wits and work as one. He called upon his gifted advisors, the wise turtles, to devise a strategy to defeat Viperox's army.

The turtles came up with a plan that would exploit the serpents' weakness—their inability to maneuver efficiently on land. With this knowledge, the Frog Army prepared for the battle that would determine the fate of Frognar.

As the sun dipped below the horizon, the Frog Army assembled at the edge of the marshes. Their eyes gleamed with determination, and their hearts beat as one. Aelius, with a gentle croak, rallied his troops, reminding them of their shared purpose and the strength they derived from unity.

The battle was fierce, and the marshlands trembled with the clash of frogs and serpents. But the Frog Army executed their strategy flawlessly, darting in and out of the water, utilizing their agility to avoid the serpents' strikes, and launching counterattacks with precision.

Aelius himself engaged in a duel with the dreaded serpent lord, Viperox. Their battle was a dance of skill and cunning, but Aelius's wisdom and connection with the spirits of the marshes gave him an edge. With a mighty leap, he pinned Viperox to the ground, and with a final croak, he commanded the serpent to retreat.

Viperox's army, defeated and demoralized, slithered away from Frognar, never to be seen again. The land rejoiced, and the creatures of Frognar hailed Aelius as their hero and the savior of their homeland.

From that day forward, the legend of the Frog Emperor and his Frog Army grew, becoming a cherished tale passed down through the generations. The spirit of unity, wisdom, and compassion embodied by Aelius and his followers continued to inspire the frogs of Frognar, reminding them that together, they were invincible, and with the bond of unity, they could overcome any challenge that came their way.

The Ammoment People

In a distant land shrouded in mystery, the legend of the Ammoment people had been passed down through generations. Their tale spoke of a unique belief known as "Trancedency." The Ammoment people inhabited a lush valley surrounded by towering mountains, and they were deeply connected to nature and the cosmos.

According to the legend, the Ammoment people believed that each individual possessed a special connection with the universe, and through a state of deep meditation and trance-like experiences, they could tap into this cosmic energy. This state of Trancedency allowed them to gain profound insights, communicate with the spirits of nature, and unlock hidden talents and abilities within themselves.

Among the Ammoment people, there was a young woman named Elara, who was known for her unyielding curiosity and her thirst for knowledge about Trancedency. Since she was a child, Elara had felt a pull towards the mystic arts and an unexplainable connection with the world around her.

As she grew older, Elara sought the wisdom of the village elders, hoping to learn more about Trancedency. They taught her ancient rituals, the art of meditation, and the ways to attune herself with the rhythms of the universe. But despite their teachings, Elara felt that there was something missing—a deeper understanding that she could not grasp.

One night, as the full moon illuminated the valley, Elara ventured alone into the heart of the Enchanted Grove, a sacred place of tranquility where the Ammoment people believed the spirits of nature resided. She sat beneath an ancient tree and began her meditation, seeking to unlock the secrets of Trancedency.

In her state of deep trance, Elara felt an ethereal presence surrounding her. The sounds of nature seemed to harmonize with her breath, and the rustling leaves seemed to whisper ancient secrets. As she opened her mind and heart, the cosmic energy flowed through her, creating a profound connection with the universe.

In this moment of transcendence, Elara experienced visions of the past, present, and future merging into one. She saw the interconnectedness of all living beings and how their actions rippled through the fabric of time. The universe spoke to her through symbols and colors, revealing the wisdom of ages.

When Elara returned from her trance, she was filled with awe and wonder at the revelations she had witnessed. She knew that her understanding of Trancedency had deepened, and she felt a profound responsibility to share this newfound knowledge with her people.

Elara began to teach others about the path of Trancedency. She held gatherings in the Enchanted Grove, guiding the Ammoment people in meditation and encouraging them to embrace their unique connections with the cosmos. As more individuals experienced moments of transcendence, the village flourished with a newfound sense of harmony and unity.

The legend of the Ammoment people and their belief in Trancedency spread beyond their valley. Travelers from distant lands journeyed to learn from Elara and her people, seeking enlightenment and inner peace. The once secluded village became a hub of spiritual seekers, drawn by the profound wisdom and serenity that emanated from the Ammoment people.

And so, the legend of the Ammoment people and their belief in Trancedency lived on, inspiring generations to embrace the cosmic energy within and to seek a deeper understanding of their place in the vast tapestry of the universe. The valley remained a place of enlightenment and wonder, where the whispers of nature and the cosmos continued to guide those who sought truth and connection.

MC Tavern Legend on Four Wheels

In the heart of the bustling city, there lived a legend on four wheels—MC Tavern, the master of car drifting. From a young age, MC was drawn to the adrenaline rush of speed and the beauty of controlled chaos on the asphalt. He grew up in the shadow of his father's garage, where he learned the art of automotive craftsmanship. But it wasn't until he discovered the art of drifting that his life took a thrilling turn.

As MC Tavern hit his late teens, he entered the underground world of street racing. He quickly gained a reputation as a fierce and skilled driver, leaving his opponents in awe as he gracefully maneuvered his car through sharp corners and hairpin turns. His style was unique, and he seemed to dance with his car, defying the laws of physics.

Word of MC Tavern's extraordinary skills spread like wildfire, attracting the attention of the city's drifting community. The mysterious drifter became a local legend, with whispers of his prowess echoing through the racing circles. But MC was more than just a talented driver; he was also a modest and kind-hearted soul.

One evening, as MC prepared for a street race, he noticed a young boy named Jake standing nearby, gazing at the race cars with wide-eyed wonder. Jake had always dreamed of being a racer, but he lacked the resources and mentorship to make that dream come true. MC Tavern saw himself in the young boy, remembering the days when he was just a dreamer with no means to pursue his passion.

Approaching Jake, MC Tavern smiled warmly and struck up a conversation. He learned about the boy's aspirations and instantly felt a connection. From that moment on, MC decided to take Jake under his wing and become his mentor, just as his father had done for him.

Over time, MC Tavern and Jake formed a bond that extended beyond drifting. MC shared life lessons, teaching Jake about respect, responsibility, and humility. He taught him that drifting was not just about speed and stunts, but also about respecting the road and other drivers. Together, they worked on Jake's driving skills, and under MC's guidance, Jake improved immensely.

As the years passed, MC Tavern's fame as a legendary drifter only grew, but he remained humble and down-to-earth. He participated in numerous competitions, showcasing his unparalleled talent, and even won several prestigious drifting championships. However, what mattered most to him was the impact he had on others, especially on young dreamers like Jake.

One day, a renowned car manufacturer invited MC Tavern to test-drive their latest model. The event was held at a professional racing circuit, and MC was eager to put the car through its paces. But he had one condition—he wanted Jake to join him on the track.

The manufacturer agreed, and as the crowd gathered to witness the spectacle, MC Tavern and Jake took to the circuit. Their synchronized moves and flawless drifts mesmerized everyone present. The event was a testament to MC's passion for mentoring and his unwavering dedication to the sport.

From that day on, MC Tavern's legend transcended beyond his drifting skills. He became a symbol of inspiration, proving that greatness wasn't just about individual achievements but also about uplifting others and leaving a positive impact on their lives.

As the years rolled by, MC Tavern eventually retired from professional drifting, but his legacy lived on. He opened a drifting school and dedicated himself to nurturing the talents of young racers, passing on his knowledge and passion for the sport to the next generation.

And so, the legend of MC Tavern, the master drifter, lives on, not just in the annals of racing history but also in the hearts of those he inspired to chase their dreams and conquer the road with unwavering determination.

The Legend of Zach

Once upon a time in the quiet village of Eldermont, there lived a young boy named Zach. He was known for his mischievous nature, always getting into trouble with his pranks and antics. But despite his playful demeanor, Zach had a heart full of courage and a thirst for adventure that couldn't be quenched.

One fateful day, as the village celebrated the annual Harvest Festival, a wise old man named Silas gathered everyone around the bonfire to share a legendary tale. He spoke of a mystical treasure hidden deep within the Forbidden Forest, a treasure said to grant unimaginable power to its possessor. Many had sought it in the past, but none had returned.

Intrigued by the tale, Zach couldn't resist the call of adventure. As the festival concluded, he bid his parents farewell and set off on his journey into the Forbidden Forest. Armed with nothing but his wits and an old map he had discovered hidden beneath his bed, he ventured into the dense foliage.

The forest was eerie and filled with whispers, and the branches seemed to reach out to him like skeletal fingers. But Zach pressed on, undeterred by the foreboding atmosphere. As he delved deeper, he encountered strange creatures and faced perilous challenges, but his determination never wavered.

Days turned into weeks, and Zach grew tired and disheartened. Doubts began to creep into his mind, but just as he was about to turn back, he stumbled upon a hidden glade bathed in ethereal light. At its center stood a magnificent tree, its trunk shimmering with an otherworldly glow.

As Zach approached, a voice echoed through the glade, gentle yet commanding. "Only the one pure of heart can claim the treasure," it whispered. Zach understood the test before him. With a steady hand and unwavering belief, he placed his hand upon the trunk, and the tree responded, revealing a hidden chamber filled with precious gemstones and artifacts.

Zach's eyes widened in awe as he beheld the riches before him. But his heart told him that true power lay not in material possessions but in the love and kindness he could share with others. Gathering only a small trinket as a token of his achievement, he left the rest behind, knowing that it belonged to a different kind of legend.

As Zach emerged from the Forbidden Forest, he returned to Eldermont as a changed young man. The village marveled at his transformation, for he carried himself with newfound wisdom and compassion. He shared his tale, emphasizing the importance of inner strength and the treasures found within one's heart.

From that day forward, the legend of Zach spread far and wide. He became a symbol of hope and inspiration, reminding others that the greatest adventures are not always found in distant lands but within ourselves. Eldermont prospered under Zach's guidance, and his legacy lived on for generations to come, reminding all who heard his story to seek their own inner treasures and embrace the power of kindness and love.

Moon Girl

In the year 1930, nestled within the small town of Crescentville, there lived a young woman named Luna. She was known throughout the town for her ethereal beauty, her eyes sparkling like moonlit skies, and her silver hair cascading down her shoulders like a gentle waterfall. Luna's grace and charm captivated the hearts of everyone who laid eyes on her, earning her the moniker "Moon Girl."

Legend had it that Moon Girl hailed from the moon itself, sent as a celestial emissary to bring light and wonder to the people of Earth. Whispers of her origin spread like wildfire, enchanting the townsfolk with tales of her moonlit adventures and mystical abilities.

The townspeople, filled with curiosity and longing, yearned to catch a glimpse of Moon Girl's luminous presence. Every evening, as the sun dipped below the horizon, they would gather at the edge of town, hoping to witness her arrival. They believed that Moon Girl would descend from the heavens in a shimmering moonbeam, gracing them with her radiant presence.

One night, as the moon hung full and bright in the sky, a young man named Henry found himself drawn to the outskirts of Crescentville. With a heart filled with longing, he joined the crowd, hoping to catch a glimpse of the legendary Moon Girl. As the anticipation grew, a hush fell over the crowd, and a faint glow began to shimmer on the horizon.

In that moment, Luna emerged, her presence illuminating the darkness. She moved with an otherworldly grace, casting a silvery glow that enchanted everyone present. The onlookers gasped in awe, mesmerized by her beauty and the mystical aura that surrounded her.

Henry couldn't help but feel an instant connection to Moon Girl. Her gaze seemed to linger on him, as if she sensed his pure heart and genuine intentions. Emboldened by this ethereal encounter, he stepped forward, taking her hand in his. In that moment, he felt a surge of warmth and love, as if the moon itself had granted him its blessings.

Their love story blossomed, transcending the boundaries of Earth and moon. Henry and Luna's bond grew stronger with each passing day, as they explored the world together, sharing their hopes and dreams. Luna, with her gentle spirit and profound wisdom, inspired Henry to become the best version of himself.

As the years went by, the legend of Moon Girl lived on, a tale of love and wonder that fascinated generations. Crescentville became a symbol of romance and enchantment, drawing countless visitors who sought to experience the magic that had unfolded within its borders.

And in the quiet moments of the night, when the moon shone brightest, it was said that Luna's spirit would grace the town once more, casting her gentle light upon all who believed in the power of love. For in the legend of Moon Girl, hope and beauty intertwined, reminding humanity of the extraordinary possibilities that lay within their reach.

Ashani the Girl in Love with the Moon

In a quaint little village nestled between rolling hills, there lived a young girl named Emily. She possessed a heart full of wonder and a mind filled with dreams that seemed to reach far beyond the horizon. Among all the wonders of the world, her heart was most captivated by the moon.

Every night, as the moonlight bathed the village in its gentle glow, Emily would gaze up at the sky, her eyes sparkling with fascination. She would spend hours beneath its luminous gaze, whispering secrets and pouring out her deepest desires, for the moon felt like a dear friend, a confidant who listened intently to her every word.

As time went by, Emily's affection for the moon grew into something deeper, something she couldn't quite explain. Her heart swelled with a love so pure and radiant that it surpassed the boundaries of reality. And so, she made a heartfelt wish: to marry the moon and spend eternity in its embrace.

Word of Emily's extraordinary love for the moon spread through the village like wildfire. Some laughed and dismissed it as childish fancy, while others marveled at the innocence and devotion of her affection. But Emily remained steadfast in her belief, determined to find a way to unite with her celestial love.

One day, a wise old woman named Clara, known for her mystical knowledge, heard of Emily's longing. Intrigued by the girl's unwavering love, Clara approached her and shared a secret she had guarded for years—a secret about the magical powers of true love.

According to Clara, if one's love for another is pure and unwavering, the universe conspires to bring them together, even if it seems impossible. Inspired by Clara's words, Emily's hope soared to new heights.

Guided by her unwavering faith, Emily embarked on a journey to seek the moon's blessing. With Clara's guidance, she climbed the highest mountains, crossed the widest oceans, and traversed dense forests. She faced countless obstacles and challenges along the way, but her love for the moon propelled her forward, undeterred.

Finally, on a clear, starlit night, Emily reached the peak of the tallest mountain. The moon stood radiant and full, casting its shimmering light upon her. Overwhelmed with joy, she poured out her heart, confessing her love and longing to marry the moon.

In that moment, as if in response to her ardent plea, the moon's light grew brighter and began to descend. A celestial beam enveloped Emily, lifting her gently towards the heavens. She felt weightless and embraced by an indescribable warmth as she ascended, her love for the moon guiding her path.

And there, amidst the stars and constellations, Emily found herself face to face with the moon, their love entwined in a celestial dance. The moon, moved by her unwavering devotion, bestowed upon her a radiant crown and a shimmering gown, symbolizing their eternal bond.

The people of the village, who had followed Emily's journey with bated breath, witnessed this miraculous union from afar. They rejoiced, their hearts filled with awe and delight. It was a testament to the power of love and the extraordinary possibilities that lay within the realm of dreams.

From that day forward, Emily and the moon became a beacon of love and hope. Their story inspired generations to cherish the depths of their hearts and believe in the power of their dreams. And every night, as the moon's gentle light bathed the village, the people would look up and remember the girl who dared to love the moon, forever grateful for the reminder that love knows no bounds and can make even the most impossible dreams come true.

The Moon Monkeys

In the dense jungles of Borneo, where ancient trees reached toward the heavens and mysterious creatures roamed, there existed a legend whispered among the indigenous people—a legend of the Moon Monkeys.

According to the tales, the Moon Monkeys were born from a cosmic union between the moon and the spirits of the forest. They possessed the ability to harness the moon's radiant energy, granting them exceptional agility and intelligence. It was said that these moonlit creatures would appear only during the full moon, dancing among the treetops and casting enchanting shadows upon the forest floor.

Among the villagers of a small tribal community nestled in the heart of Borneo, a young girl named Maya was known for her unwavering curiosity and adventurous spirit. Fascinated by the stories of the Moon Monkeys, she yearned to witness their magical dance beneath the moonlit canopy.

On a fateful night, as the full moon illuminated the sky, Maya slipped away from the village. Guided by her intuition and an insatiable desire to uncover the truth, she ventured deep into the lush jungle, her footsteps barely making a sound upon the earth.

As Maya continued her nocturnal exploration, a soft melody carried by the gentle breeze reached her ears.

Mesmerized, she followed the enchanting sound, its ethereal quality drawing her closer to the moonlit clearing ahead.

There, amid a kaleidoscope of moonbeams filtering through the canopy, Maya's eyes widened in wonder. The Moon Monkeys, with their shimmering silver fur and nimble limbs, leaped from branch to branch, their movements synchronized to the rhythm of the night.

Transfixed by their graceful dance, Maya felt an overwhelming sense of harmony and unity with the natural world. She watched in awe as the Moon Monkeys leaped higher and higher, their silhouettes etching fleeting patterns against the starry canvas above.

Unexpectedly, one of the Moon Monkeys locked eyes with Maya, its silver gaze brimming with recognition. With a mischievous grin, it beckoned her to join their celestial ballet. Overcome with excitement, Maya summoned all her courage and leaped from the ground, defying gravity as she soared among the treetops.

In that magical moment, Maya became one with the Moon Monkeys. The moon's energy coursed through her veins, granting her the grace and agility of her new companions. Together, they twirled and spun, their collective energy painting an ethereal tapestry of beauty and wonder.

As the night waned, the Moon Monkeys gently guided Maya back to the forest floor, their dance coming to a close. They bid her farewell with a silent understanding, their silver eyes conveying the depth of their connection.

Maya returned to the village, her heart brimming with the magic of her encounter. With newfound wisdom and reverence for the natural world, she shared her extraordinary tale with her people. The legend of the Moon Monkeys became a cherished part of their culture, reminding them of the delicate balance between mankind and the enchanting spirits that dwelled in the heart of the jungle.

And every full moon thereafter, the people of Borneo would gather beneath the ancient trees, their eyes fixed on the luminous night sky. They would whisper tales of the Moon Monkeys and honor the moon's brilliance, knowing that its ethereal light connected them to the mystical wonders of their beloved homeland.

Deep within the lush rainforests of Sumatra, a land of breathtaking beauty and rich biodiversity, there existed a legend of an ethereal being known as the Sumatra Angel. The legend spoke of a mystical creature with wings as vibrant as the tropical flowers and a voice that could soothe even the wildest of beasts.

It was said that the Sumatra Angel was a guardian spirit of the land, entrusted with the task of preserving the delicate balance between humans and nature. Only those with pure hearts and a genuine love for the natural world could catch a glimpse of this majestic being.

In a humble village nestled on the outskirts of the rainforest, lived a young girl named Aria. Aria possessed an extraordinary connection with nature, spending her days exploring the forest's hidden wonders and listening to the whispers of the ancient trees. She had heard tales of the Sumatra Angel from her elders, and her heart yearned to witness its ethereal presence.

Driven by her insatiable curiosity, Aria ventured deeper into the rainforest, her steps guided by an invisible hand that seemed to know the way. The forest enveloped her in its emerald embrace, its scents and sounds becoming a symphony of life.

Days turned into weeks, and Aria's unwavering determination remained steadfast. She braved treacherous paths, faced wild creatures with gentle respect, and communed with the spirits of the forest. She would not rest until she encountered the legendary Sumatra Angel.

One evening, as the sun dipped below the horizon, casting a golden glow upon the rainforest, Aria stumbled upon a hidden glade. Bathed in the soft light of the setting sun, a figure emerged—a being of radiant beauty, its wings adorned with hues of emerald and sapphire.

The Sumatra Angel extended a hand, and Aria, overcome with awe and reverence, approached with a mix of excitement and trepidation. The angel's voice resonated like a gentle breeze through the treetops as it spoke to Aria, whispering words of ancient wisdom and sharing the secrets of the rainforest.

With every passing moment, Aria felt a deep connection forming between her and the Sumatra Angel. She realized that the angel was not merely a guardian of the land, but a reflection of the love and respect she herself had for nature. It was a profound reminder that the bond between humans and the environment was a sacred responsibility.

As dawn broke, the Sumatra Angel spread its wings, ready to depart. Aria, filled with gratitude and a sense of purpose, knew that her encounter with this mystical being had changed her forever. With renewed determination, she vowed to be an ambassador for the rainforest, protecting and preserving its beauty for generations to come.

Word of Aria's encounter with the Sumatra Angel spread throughout the village, igniting a spark of reverence for the natural world. The villagers recognized the importance of nurturing their environment and living in harmony with the creatures that called it home.

In time, the Sumatra Angel became a symbol of hope and stewardship, a guiding light for those who sought to protect the rainforest's delicate ecosystem. And whenever a gentle breeze rustled through the forest, the whispers of the angel could still be heard, reminding all who listened that the true magic of Sumatra lay not just in its lush greenery, but in the hearts of those who cherished its splendor.

Moon Frogs

In the heart of the enchanting Sumatra forest, where ancient trees reached towards the sky and a symphony of wildlife echoed through the lush greenery, there existed a mystical species known as moon frogs. Legends whispered among the indigenous people spoke of their magical abilities and their connection to the moon.

Moon frogs were unlike any other amphibians that graced the forest floor. Their radiant skin shimmered with a soft luminescence, reminiscent of the moon's gentle glow. It was said that during the full moon, when the night sky was at its brightest, these extraordinary creatures would gather near the moonlit streams to perform a mesmerizing dance.

In a small village on the outskirts of the Sumatra forest, a young girl named Amara lived with an unyielding curiosity and love for nature. She had heard the tales of the moon frogs from her grandparents, who spoke of their elegance and the ethereal melodies that accompanied their enchanting dance. Amara dreamed of witnessing the moon frogs in their full glory.

One night, as the full moon bathed the forest in its silvery light, Amara embarked on a nocturnal adventure. Guided by the whispers of the wind and the secrets of the ancient trees, she ventured deeper into the heart of the Sumatra forest. The sounds of nocturnal creatures filled the air, and the moon cast long, mystical shadows upon her path.

As Amara moved through the dense undergrowth, a soft croaking melody reached her ears. Her heart leaped with excitement, for she recognized the distinct call of the moon frogs. Following the melodic tune, she arrived at a moonlit clearing beside a glistening stream.

There, she beheld a breathtaking sight. Moon frogs of various sizes and colors emerged from the shadows, their luminous bodies illuminating the clearing with their gentle radiance. They hopped and leaped with unparalleled grace, creating ripples in the moonlit waters and casting shimmering reflections upon the surrounding foliage.

Amara stood in awe, her eyes sparkling with wonder. The air was filled with the soft melodies of the moon frogs, creating a symphony that seemed to harmonize with the rustling leaves and the gentle whispers of the forest spirits.

With a sense of reverence and admiration, Amara approached the moon frogs, careful not to disrupt their dance. The creatures, sensing her genuine appreciation and respect, allowed her to be a part of their moonlit celebration. Amara joined them in their intricate movements, twirling and spinning beneath the watchful gaze of the moon.

As the night wore on, the moon frogs gradually returned to the shadows, bidding Amara farewell with a chorus of farewell croaks. She watched them disappear into the depths of the forest, their magical presence etched into her memory forever.

Amara returned to her village, bursting with excitement and a newfound appreciation for the beauty of nature. She shared her encounter with the moon frogs with her fellow villagers, recounting the mystical dance and the serenade that had captured her heart.

From that day forward, the village celebrated the moon frogs as symbols of harmony and wonder. They recognized the importance of preserving the delicate ecosystem of the Sumatra forest, ensuring that the moon frogs and their enchanting dance would be cherished by generations to come.

And as the moon reached its fullest phase each month, the villagers would gather near the moonlit streams, their hearts filled with anticipation. They would listen for the soft melodies of the moon frogs, knowing that in their presence, they would find a connection to the moon and a reminder of the extraordinary magic that thrived in the Sumatra forest.

Stairway to Heaven

In the picturesque town of Manali, nestled amidst the majestic Himalayas, there existed a legend whispered among the locals—a legend of a stairway to heaven. It was said that hidden within the depths of the towering mountains, there lay a mystical path that led to a realm of unimaginable beauty and serenity.

Among the residents of Manali, there lived a young woman named Kavya. She possessed a heart filled with curiosity and an unquenchable thirst for adventure. Drawn to the whispers of the stairway to heaven, Kavya yearned to uncover the truth behind the legend and experience the wonders that awaited beyond mortal realms.

Guided by an unyielding spirit and armed with little more than her courage, Kavya embarked on a journey to seek the stairway to heaven. She ventured deep into the rugged terrain, her steps determined and unwavering. The air grew crisp, and the snow-capped peaks watched over her as silent guardians.

Days turned into weeks as Kavya climbed higher and higher, overcoming treacherous slopes and bone-chilling winds. She faced numerous challenges, but her determination pushed her forward, her heart filled with the promise of discovering the stairway to heaven.

And then, one fateful morning, as the sun painted the sky in hues of gold, Kavya reached a hidden valley. Before her eyes, a sight unfolded that took her breath away—a magnificent staircase, spiraling upwards towards the heavens, carved from pure crystal. Each step glimmered with a divine radiance, casting a soft ethereal glow upon the surroundings.

With a mixture of awe and anticipation, Kavya ascended the staircase, her senses heightened with the promise of an extraordinary destination. Each step she took filled her with a sense of tranquility and a profound connection to the mystical forces that governed the universe.

As Kavya continued her ascent, the air grew lighter, carrying the scent of flowers that seemed to bloom in the heavens. Melodies of unseen birds echoed in harmony, and a gentle breeze brushed against her skin like a caress.

Finally, at the pinnacle of the stairway, Kavya beheld a sight that transcended the boundaries of imagination. She found herself in a realm of indescribable beauty—a land where emerald meadows stretched into eternity, where rivers flowed with waters that shimmered like liquid silver, and where the sky radiated a kaleidoscope of colors.

In this heavenly abode, Kavya felt a sense of profound peace and pure joy envelop her being. She realized that the stairway to heaven was not just a physical journey, but a transformation of the spirit—a glimpse into the boundless possibilities of love, harmony, and enlightenment.

Overwhelmed by the magnitude of her experience, Kavya made a promise to herself. She vowed to carry the essence of this celestial realm within her heart, and to spread love, kindness, and compassion to all she encountered on her return to the earthly realm.

With a contented smile and a heart full of gratitude, Kavya descended the crystal stairs, back to the earthly realm of Manali. Her presence radiated an otherworldly glow, and those who crossed her path felt a sense of serenity and wonder.

The legend of the stairway to heaven lived on, a reminder to the people of Manali and beyond that the path to enlightenment and true happiness lay not in physical realms, but in the depths of one's soul. And in the quiet moments, as the sun dipped below the horizon and painted the sky in hues of gold, the people of Manali would gaze towards the mountains, knowing that somewhere within their midst, the stairway to heaven awaited those with pure hearts and unwavering spirits.

Tale of the Sun God

In the ancient kingdom of Jawa, nestled on the lush island of Java in Indonesia, a legendary tale of the Sun God was told through generations. It was a time when kingdoms flourished and mythical beings were believed to roam the land, bridging the realms of mortals and deities.

In the year 1533, during the reign of the great King Arjuna, the kingdom of Jawa faced a grave threat. A prolonged drought had plagued the land, crops withered, and the people suffered under the scorching sun. Prayers and rituals were performed, but the gods seemed distant, their benevolence withheld.

In this time of desperate need, a young and courageous warrior named Aditya emerged from the village of Pura. Aditya possessed an unwavering spirit and a heart that burned with a desire to save his people. Driven by an unyielding determination, he embarked on a quest to seek the aid of the Sun God.

Guided by ancient scriptures and whispered tales, Aditya trekked through the dense jungles and rugged mountains of Java. His path was treacherous, fraught with perils and mystical creatures, but he pressed on, his faith fueling his every step.

After weeks of arduous travel, Aditya reached the sacred peak of Mount Merapi. Standing tall and resolute, he raised his arms towards the heavens and called upon the Sun God, his voice reverberating through the valleys and canyons.

Suddenly, a blinding light pierced through the sky, casting a radiant glow upon Aditya. The ground beneath him trembled, and from the center of the light emerged a majestic figure—an ethereal being, shimmering with the brilliance of a thousand suns.

It was Surya, the Sun God, adorned in golden armor, his chariot of fire drawn by celestial horses. His presence filled the air with warmth and divine energy, and his voice boomed like thunder as he addressed Aditya.

"You have shown unwavering devotion, young warrior," Surya declared. "Your heart burns with the same intensity as my fiery rays. I shall grant your request."

With a wave of his hand, Surya commanded the heavens to open. Rain fell in gentle cascades, quenching the parched land and rejuvenating the earth. Lush greenery sprouted, and the cries of joy echoed through the kingdom of Jawa.

Surya bestowed upon Aditya a sacred relic—a golden amulet that held the power of the sun. This talisman would forever connect Aditya to the divine forces, enabling him to bring light and hope to his people.

News of Aditya's encounter with the Sun God spread throughout the land, and the people hailed him as a hero. Aditya, humbled by the experience, dedicated his life to serving his kingdom, ensuring the prosperity and well-being of his people.

From that day forward, the legend of the Sun God and the warrior Aditya echoed through the ages. Every year, on the anniversary of the great drought, the people of Jawa celebrated with a grand festival, honoring the Sun God's benevolence and Aditya's bravery.

And amidst the festivities, as the sun bathed the land in its golden embrace, the people of Jawa would gather, their hearts filled with gratitude, knowing that their beloved Sun God would forever shine upon them, bestowing warmth, abundance, and eternal light upon the kingdom of Jawa.

Dog Heaven

In the enchanting land of Jawa, on the mystical island of Java in Indonesia, a heartwarming legend echoed through the villages—a legend that spoke of a special place called "Dog Heaven." It was believed that when a dog's time on Earth came to an end, their spirits would ascend to this heavenly realm, where they would frolic and play, forever surrounded by love and happiness.

In a small village nestled in the countryside, there lived a kind-hearted woman named Lila. She had a deep love for animals, especially dogs. Her home was a sanctuary for stray and abandoned canines, and she cared for them with unwavering compassion.

Among her many beloved dogs was Budi, a playful and loyal companion. Budi had spent his days by Lila's side, bringing joy and laughter to the village with his boundless energy and wagging tail. The villagers admired the special bond between Lila and Budi, and they often remarked that when the time came, Budi would surely find his way to Dog Heaven.

One sunny day, as Budi frolicked in the village square, a tragic accident occurred. Budi's life was cut short, leaving Lila and the entire village devastated. Tears fell like raindrops, and sorrow filled the air as they mourned the loss of their dear friend.

But amidst the grief, a whisper of hope fluttered through the village. It was said that when a dog's spirit departed from the earthly realm, a celestial path would appear—a path that led directly to the gates of Dog Heaven. Inspired by this belief, the villagers gathered, vowing to guide Budi's spirit on his journey.

As the sun dipped below the horizon, casting an ethereal glow upon the village, Lila and the villagers set out on their solemn mission. They walked through fields and forests, guided by the twinkling stars above, until they reached a meadow enveloped in moonlight.

There, at the edge of the meadow, a gentle breeze brushed against their faces. They watched in awe as the breeze shaped itself into a luminous path, stretching towards the heavens. It was the celestial route to Dog Heaven—a stairway of light that beckoned Budi's spirit to ascend.

With love and reverence, Lila stepped forward, carrying Budi's spirit in her heart. The villagers followed, their hearts brimming with sorrow and gratitude for the joy Budi had brought into their lives.

As they ascended the celestial stairway, a chorus of barks and wagging tails greeted them. They had arrived at Dog Heaven—a realm of endless green meadows, crystal-clear streams, and dogs of all shapes and sizes frolicking joyfully.

Budi's spirit was welcomed with open paws. The villagers watched as he joined the playful pack, his spirit glowing with happiness. In Dog Heaven, every dog found their forever home, their spirits forever young and vibrant.

Lila and the villagers bid their final farewells, knowing that Budi was in a place of eternal joy. They returned to the village with heavy hearts but filled with a sense of peace, knowing that their dear friend had found his way to the celestial paradise promised by the legend.

From that day forward, the villagers of Jawa celebrated the bond between humans and dogs with a special ceremony. Every year, on a moonlit night, they gathered to honor the dogs that had departed, lighting lanterns and sending their love and gratitude towards the heavens.

And in the quiet moments of the night, when the moon bathed the land in its gentle glow, the villagers would look up, knowing that Dog Heaven awaited their faithful companions. They found solace in the legend that assured them that all dogs, like Budi, would forever find their way to that wondrous place, where they would play, chase their tails, and bask in eternal love.

The Magnetite

Deep within the dense and mysterious Jim Corbett Forest, where ancient trees whispered secrets and sunlight filtered through the thick foliage, a legend spoke of a remarkable creature known as the Magnetite. It was said to be a small and elusive creature with the extraordinary ability to control and manipulate magnetic fields.

According to the legends, the Maganitite possessed a coat of shimmering iridescent hues, reflecting the vibrant colors of the forest. Its eyes gleamed with an otherworldly intensity, harboring the power to attract and repel with a mere gaze. The Maganitite's magnetic prowess could draw metals towards it or repulse them with a simple flick of its tail.

Among the residents of the nearby village, stories of the Maganitite were passed down through generations. The creature was believed to be a guardian of the forest, protecting its delicate ecosystem and ensuring the harmony between nature and mankind.

In this village lived a young boy named Raju, whose heart brimmed with curiosity and a deep love for the natural world. Raju spent his days exploring the depths of the Jim Corbett Forest, captivated by its wonders and secrets. The legend of the Maganitite fascinated him, and he longed to catch a glimpse of this extraordinary creature.

One day, as Raju ventured deep into the heart of the forest, his senses heightened, and a magnetic energy seemed to pulse through the air. Guided by an invisible force, he followed the magnetic pull, his heart pounding with anticipation.

As he delved deeper, Raju discovered a hidden clearing where the forest seemed to hum with a magnetic aura. In the center stood the Magnetite, its shimmering form casting an ethereal glow. Raju's eyes widened with awe and wonder.

Approaching with cautious steps, Raju found himself within the magnetic field of the Maganitite. He felt an invisible force tugging at him, a sensation that seemed to awaken a dormant power within his own being.

The Magnetite regarded Raju with intelligent eyes, acknowledging his pure heart and love for the forest. It understood his longing to connect with the natural world and share in its magic. With a gentle flick of its tail, the Maganitite invited Raju to explore the depths of its magnetic domain.

Under the Magnetite's guidance, Raju discovered his own magnetic abilities. He could attract and repel objects, bend iron and steel with his touch, and feel the magnetic pulse of the Earth beneath his feet. The Maganitite became Raju's mentor, teaching him the delicate balance of power and responsibility that came with these extraordinary gifts.

Days turned into months as Raju honed his newfound skills, his bond with the Maganitite growing stronger. Together, they ensured the harmony of the forest, protecting its treasures and guiding lost animals back to safety.

News of Raju and his connection to the Maganitite spread throughout the village. The villagers marveled at his magnetic abilities and regarded him as a guardian of their beloved forest. Raju, humbled by their admiration, continued his mission to protect and preserve the Jim Corbett Forest.

As the years passed, Raju became a symbol of the legend of the Maganitite—a reminder of the extraordinary powers that lay within the depths of nature. He shared his knowledge with the villagers, inspiring them to appreciate and cherish the delicate balance between mankind and the natural world.

And in the depths of the Jim Corbett Forest, the legend of the Maganitite lived on, whispering tales of magnetic wonders and the profound connection between humans and the forces of nature. The forest thrived under Raju's guardianship, its beauty and harmony forever intertwined with the magnetic energy that pulsed through its ancient trees.

Maroi Sun

In the vast landscapes of New Zealand, where rolling hills met pristine beaches and misty mountains stood tall, there existed a tale of great peril and courage—a legend of the Sun's capture and the hero known as the Maroi Man who embarked on a quest to free it.

Long ago, the Sun held a vital place in the lives of the Maroi people. It provided warmth, light, and energy, nourishing their land and spirits. But one fateful day, darkness descended upon the land as an evil sorceress named Morgana cast a powerful spell, capturing the Sun within a celestial prison.

As the world plunged into darkness, the Maroi people grew despondent, their crops withering and their spirits waning. In this time of despair, a young Maroi warrior named Tane rose from the ranks. Tane possessed a noble heart and unwavering determination, driven by a deep love for his people and the land they called home.

Guided by ancient legends and the whispers of his ancestors, Tane set forth on a perilous journey to free the Sun. He traversed rugged terrains, crossed treacherous rivers, and climbed towering mountains, his every step fuelled by the hope of restoring light and life to his people.

Finally, after enduring countless challenges, Tane reached the heart of Morgana's domain—a forbidding fortress perched atop a mist-shrouded peak. With courage coursing through his veins, he confronted the sorceress, demanding the release of the Sun.

Morgana, wicked and powerful, scoffed at Tane's audacity. She taunted him with her dark magic, attempting to break his spirit. But Tane remained resolute, his unwavering belief in the goodness of the world bolstering his determination.

Undeterred, Tane delved deep into the fortress, navigating through labyrinthine passages and facing enchanted creatures that sought to thwart his progress. With each step, his spirit burned brighter, infused with the strength of his ancestors and the love of his people.

Finally, at the heart of the fortress, Tane stood before the celestial prison that held the captured Sun. With a surge of inner power, he broke through the sorceress's spell, shattering the prison and releasing the radiant Sun.

As the Sun emerged from its confinement, its golden rays pierced through the darkness, illuminating the land with a brilliance that hadn't been seen in ages. The Maroi people, filled with awe and gratitude, rejoiced as warmth and light returned to their homes.

Tane, hailed as a hero, basked in the joy of his people. He had not only freed the Sun but also rekindled hope and rejuvenated their spirits. His selfless act of bravery had woven a new chapter in the legend of the Maroi people—a tale of courage, resilience, and the triumph of light over darkness.

From that day forward, Tane was revered as the Maroi Man, a symbol of bravery and the embodiment of their indomitable spirit. The legend of his heroic quest echoed through the generations, a reminder to the Maroi people and all who heard the tale of the power that lies within each individual to dispel darkness and restore light.

And in the breathtaking landscapes of New Zealand, where the Sun's rays painted the sky in hues of gold, the Maroi people continued to honor their hero, forever grateful for the renewed light and the enduring legacy of Tane, the Maroi Man who freed the Sun.

Winter Solstice Flowers

In the picturesque country of Switzerland, where snow-capped mountains kissed the sky and meandering rivers carved their way through lush valleys, there existed a mystical phenomenon—a legend of radiant flowers that bloomed in the peak of night during the winter solstice. It was said that at precisely 1 am, when the world was cloaked in darkness, these enchanting blossoms would emerge, illuminating the land with their ethereal glow.

Deep within a secluded valley, nestled between towering peaks, lay a quaint village named Edelweiss. Its inhabitants treasured the legend of the radiant flowers, eagerly anticipating their arrival each year. Among the villagers, a young girl named Emilia was captivated by the tale, her heart filled with wonder and anticipation.

As the winter solstice approached, Emilia could hardly contain her excitement. She spent her days gathering stories and researching the folklore surrounding the radiant flowers. Guided by her insatiable curiosity, she ventured into the depths of the valley, hoping to witness their magical beauty firsthand.

The night of the winter solstice arrived, and the village was bathed in an eerie stillness. Emilia, wrapped in warm layers, ventured out into the crisp winter air, her breath creating delicate misty clouds. She followed a hidden path that led to a meadow known to harbor the elusive flowers.

As the clock struck 1 am, the world seemed to hold its breath. Emilia's eyes widened in anticipation as she watched the meadow transform before her. Tiny buds burst open, revealing exquisite flowers that emitted a soft, radiant glow. Their petals shimmered with hues of lavender, azure, and gold, casting a gentle light upon the snow-covered landscape.

Emilia was awestruck. The meadow was transformed into a magical realm, its beauty rivaling that of fairy tales. The radiant flowers danced in the stillness of the night, their incandescent glow reflecting in Emilia's wide-eyed gaze.

Overwhelmed by the enchantment before her, Emilia stepped forward, her feet crunching lightly on the snowy ground. She reached out, delicately touching one of the blossoms. Its petals felt velvety and warm, as if they held a fragment of the sun's own essence.

In that moment, Emilia understood the true magic of the radiant flowers. They symbolized hope, resilience, and the eternal cycle of life. Amidst the cold embrace of winter, they bloomed as a reminder that even in the darkest of times, beauty and light could emerge, illuminating the path forward.

As the first rays of dawn painted the horizon, the radiant flowers began to slowly close their petals, their glow diminishing. Emilia, with a heart brimming with gratitude, bid them farewell, knowing that their beauty would return again, year after year.

Returning to the village, Emilia shared her tale with the villagers, painting a vivid picture of the breathtaking scene she had witnessed. The legend of the radiant flowers grew stronger, and each year, the villagers would gather in the meadow on the winter solstice, awaiting the magical blooming of these extraordinary blossoms.

And in the picturesque valleys of Switzerland, where snow blanketed the land and the mountains stood tall, the legend of the radiant flowers lived on. It became a reminder to all who heard the tale, that even in the coldest of winters, the light of hope and beauty would always find a way to bloom, illuminating the hearts and souls of those who believed in its magic.

Radiance Beckons

In the ancient land of Pannang, shrouded in mystery and bathed in golden sunlight, a legend whispered through the winds—a legend of the Sun's firstborn child who descended upon Earth, carrying the radiance of their celestial parent. It was said that this child possessed a divine connection to the Sun, emitting a brilliant light that beckoned all who beheld it.

In the year 1256 BC, during the reign of King Mahendra, the land of Pannang flourished. Its people revered the Sun, for it provided warmth and life to their bountiful lands. They celebrated the legend of the Sun's firstborn child, believing that their presence brought blessings and prosperity to the kingdom.

Among the people of Pannang was a young woman named Surya, whose name bore the resemblance of the Sun itself. Surya possessed a gentle spirit and an ethereal beauty that radiated from within. She was known for her kindness and wisdom, and her connection to the divine seemed to transcend mortal bounds.

One fateful day, as the sun bathed the land in its golden embrace, Surya found herself alone on a hillside overlooking the kingdom. She basked in the warm glow of the sunlight, feeling a familiar pull deep within her being. The winds whispered her name, carrying the echoes of the legend and calling her to embrace her destiny.

Guided by an invisible force, Surya embarked on a journey that would forever change her life and the fate of Pannang. She traversed through verdant forests and treacherous mountains, her heart brimming with anticipation and trepidation. With each step, her radiance grew, her connection to the Sun strengthening.

Finally, Surya arrived at an ancient temple nestled within a hidden valley. As she stepped through the hallowed entrance, a blinding light enveloped her, revealing a celestial chamber where a newborn child lay cradled in a bed of golden rays.

The child possessed an otherworldly beauty, their eyes mirroring the Sun's fiery glow. Surya knew in her heart that she had found the Sun's firstborn child—the one whose radiance would guide and inspire the kingdom of Pannang.

With tender care, Surya took the child in her arms, their essences intertwining. She named the child Alok, meaning "radiance," for they emitted a glow that rivaled the brilliance of the Sun itself.

Word of the Sun's child spread throughout Pannang, and the people rejoiced. They recognized Alok as a divine gift, a beacon of hope and light that would lead them towards a future filled with prosperity and harmony.

As Alok grew, their presence continued to illuminate the kingdom of Pannang. Their wisdom surpassed their years, their compassion touched the hearts of all, and their radiance brought joy and unity to the land.

Under Alok's guidance, Pannang flourished. Crops grew abundantly, the people prospered, and a sense of serenity settled upon the kingdom. Alok's legacy became intertwined with the legend of the Sun's firstborn child, a legend that would be passed down through generations, reminding the people of Pannang of the divine radiance that resided within them all.

And in the land of Pannang, where the golden sunsets painted the sky in hues of amber and crimson, the legacy of Alok lived on. The people remembered their connection to the Sun's firstborn child, embracing their own inner radiance and cherishing the light that illuminated their lives.

For in their hearts, they understood that the true power of the Sun's child was not simply in their celestial heritage, but in the ability of each individual to embrace their own inner radiance and share it with the world—a gift that would forever guide them towards a future filled with love, compassion, and eternal light.

The White Traveler

In the breathtaking expanse of Banff National Park, nestled among towering mountains and dense forests, a chilling legend whispered through the pines—the legend of The White Traveler. It was said that a specter, draped in a flowing white cloak, wandered the park's trails and pathways, striking fear into the hearts of those who encountered it.

In the winter of 2021, a group of adventurous hikers set out to explore Banff's untamed beauty. Their names were Rachel, Mark, and Emily, and they were drawn to the park's mystique and the promise of unforgettable experiences. Little did they know, their journey would soon take a terrifying turn.

As the trio ventured deep into the wilderness, the air grew colder, and the daylight waned. They decided to set up camp near a secluded lake, their tents surrounded by a hushed silence that seemed to deepen as night fell.

It was around midnight when Rachel, unable to sleep, peered outside her tent. She caught a glimpse of movement in the distance—an eerie figure cloaked in white, slowly gliding through the snow-covered landscape. Her heart raced, and she woke Mark and Emily, who listened with trepidation.

They cautiously stepped outside, their breath visible in the frigid air. The figure grew nearer, its ethereal presence sending shivers down their spines. Its white cloak billowed in an invisible wind, its face hidden beneath a hood of darkness.

Rachel, her voice trembling, whispered, "It's...it's The White Traveler. The legend... it's true."

The figure seemed to sense their fear, its spectral gaze fixed upon them. Without warning, it raised a pale, skeletal hand, pointing towards the depths of the forest. A bone-chilling moan emanated from its throat—a sound that reverberated through the night.

Paralyzed with terror, the trio reluctantly followed the White Traveler's gesture, the eerie specter leading them deeper into the unknown. The forest whispered secrets, its twisted branches clawing at their sanity. The temperature dropped even further, each breath hanging in the air like frozen mist.

Suddenly, a clearing emerged, bathed in an unnatural glow. The trio stood at the edge, their eyes wide with horror. In the center of the clearing stood a circle of ancient trees, their gnarled branches intertwined, forming a gateway to darkness.

The White Traveler raised its hands once more, unleashing a mournful wail that pierced the night. The ground trembled, and the gateway opened, revealing a void of shadows that seemed to swallow all light.

With a final, haunting gaze, the White Traveler vanished into the abyss, leaving the trio to confront the unknown before them. Fear clung to their souls, but their survival instincts propelled them forward.

As they crossed the threshold, a malevolent force enveloped them. Nightmarish visions twisted their minds, blurring the boundaries between reality and madness. Each step brought them deeper into a realm of nightmares, where their deepest fears manifested before their eyes.

In a desperate bid for escape, Rachel, Mark, and Emily fought against the clutches of darkness. Their resolve grew stronger, their will to survive burning like a beacon in the blackened void.

Suddenly, a blinding light erupted, piercing through the darkness. The trio shielded their eyes as the light intensified, illuminating the ethereal figure of the White Traveler. Its face, once obscured, became visible—a skeletal visage etched with sorrow.

With a voice filled with ancient wisdom, the White Traveler spoke, "You have faced your deepest fears. You have proven your strength."

The gateway closed, and the trio found themselves back in the clearing. The forest returned to a peaceful hush, the horrors of the night banished.

They exchanged glances, their hearts still pounding. Though shaken, they were forever changed by the encounter with the White Traveler. They understood that true bravery lay in confronting one's fears, in embracing the unknown, and in emerging stronger on the other side.

From that night forward, the legend of the White Traveler in Banff National Park grew, serving as a cautionary tale for those who ventured into the wilderness. The trio, forever connected by their harrowing experience, carried with them a newfound appreciation for life's fragility and the strength that lies within the human spirit.

And as hikers explored the vast beauty of Banff, they treaded cautiously, mindful of the legend that whispered through the trees—the legend of The White Traveler, a haunting reminder of the depths of darkness and the indomitable light that can emerge from its depths.

Legend of Earth

In the realm of myths and legends, where time and space intertwine, there exists a tale as old as the universe itself— the Legend of Earth. It is a story that speaks of cosmic forces, celestial beings, and the harmonious dance that gave birth to our wondrous planet.

In the vast expanse of the cosmos, a gathering of cosmic deities convened. They were the creators, the weavers of destiny, and the guardians of the cosmic balance. Among them stood Gaia, the embodiment of the Earth, and Aether, the essence of the boundless universe.

Gaia and Aether possessed a deep love for each other, their cosmic energies entwined in an eternal embrace. They yearned to manifest their love into something tangible, something that would bring beauty and life to the universe. And so, they embarked on a celestial dance, their steps synchronizing with the rhythm of creation.

With each twirl, Aether released celestial stardust, swirling and shimmering with vibrant colors. Gaia, in turn, imbued the stardust with her essence, infusing it with the power to nurture and sustain life. Together, their cosmic ballet grew more intricate and profound, shaping the destiny of the universe.

As their dance reached its climax, the stardust coalesced into a magnificent celestial sphere—the Earth. It was a world of untamed beauty, adorned with sprawling oceans, majestic mountains, and lush landscapes. Gaia's love and Aether's cosmic energy permeated every inch of this newborn planet.

The deities marveled at their creation, for it held the potential for extraordinary wonders. Gaia, with her nurturing touch, breathed life into the Earth, birthing an array of diverse and magnificent beings—the plants, the animals, and eventually, humanity.

With each passing moment, the Earth evolved and flourished. Seasons painted the land with vibrant hues, rivers carved their paths through rugged terrains, and the sky transformed with each dawn and dusk. Gaia's love for her creation was boundless, as she witnessed the cycles of life and the interconnectedness of all living things.

Through the ages, stories of the Legend of Earth were passed down, serving as a reminder of the profound bond between the planet and its inhabitants. They spoke of the responsibility entrusted upon humanity to cherish and protect the Earth—to be stewards of its resources and guardians of its delicate balance.

And so, the legend lives on, an eternal reminder that Earth is not merely a collection of rocks and oceans, but a living, breathing entity—a testament to the cosmic love of Gaia and Aether. It calls upon us, the inhabitants of this remarkable planet, to honor and preserve its beauty, to nurture the web of life that intertwines us all, and to celebrate the eternal dance of creation that brought forth our beloved home, the Earth.

Cosmic & Celestial Tales

*

The Unicorn

In the mystical depths of the Jim Corbett Forest, where ancient trees whispered secrets and sunlight danced through the foliage, a timeless legend whispered through the air—the Legend of the Unicorn. It was said that deep within the heart of the forest, a magnificent unicorn roamed, its presence embodying grace, purity, and untamed magic.

In the year 2024, as the forest bloomed with renewed vitality, a young girl named Maya found herself drawn to the legends surrounding the mythical creature. Maya possessed a heart filled with wonder and an unwavering belief in the extraordinary. She ventured into the depths of the Jim Corbett Forest, her eyes scanning the verdant landscape in search of the legendary unicorn.

Days turned into weeks as Maya explored the forest's hidden nooks and winding trails. Her heart beat with anticipation, her spirit connected to the ancient tales that spoke of the unicorn's ethereal beauty and healing powers. She remained undeterred, her determination guiding her every step.

One serene evening, as the sun began its descent, casting a golden glow upon the forest, Maya stumbled upon a hidden glade. There, bathed in soft beams of light, stood the legendary unicorn—a majestic creature with a gleaming ivory coat, a golden horn, and eyes that held the wisdom of centuries.

Maya's breath caught in her throat as she approached the creature with reverence. The unicorn regarded her with gentle eyes, its presence radiating tranquility and magic. Maya reached out, her fingers grazing the unicorn's silken mane, feeling an electric surge of energy coursing through her veins.

In that moment, an unspoken bond formed between Maya and the unicorn. It recognized her pure heart, her unwavering belief in the power of dreams, and the beauty that exists within the depths of one's spirit. The unicorn's horn emitted a soft glow, enveloping Maya in a cocoon of warmth and love.

From that day forward, Maya became a guardian of the unicorn's legend. She shared her encounter with the villagers, kindling hope and reminding them of the enchantment that lay within the depths of the forest. The unicorn became a symbol of purity, inspiration, and the transformative power of belief.

News of the legendary unicorn's presence spread throughout the land, attracting visitors from far and wide. They journeyed to the Jim Corbett Forest, their hearts open to the possibility of encountering the mythical creature and experiencing its transformative magic.

The unicorn, aware of its newfound role as a beacon of hope and wonder, continued to grace the forest with its presence. It ventured beyond the hidden glade, roaming freely among the trees, its radiant energy infusing the air with a sense of awe and harmony.

And in the forest of Jim Corbett, where ancient trees whispered secrets and sunlight filtered through the canopy, the Legend of the Unicorn lived on. It served as a reminder to all who entered the forest—whether seeking enchantment, solace, or a connection to the magic that resides within— that dreams are within reach, and that the power of belief can illuminate even the darkest of paths.

Brahmaputra

In the ancient land of India, nestled amidst lush greenery and flowing rivers, a tale of wonder and intrigue was passed down through generations—a legend known as the Legend of Brahmaputra. It was a tale that spoke of a mystical river, a source of both blessings and perils, set in the year 1200 BC.

In a small village nestled in the heart of India, a young student named Arjun sat at the feet of his wise teacher, Guru Rajan. Arjun was eager to learn, his mind thirsty for knowledge and his heart open to the wisdom of the ages. As the evening sun bathed the village in a golden hue, Guru Rajan began to tell him the legendary tale.

"Long ago," Guru Rajan began, "there flowed a river named Bhramapurta. It was said to possess extraordinary powers, capable of granting blessings to those who approached it with a pure heart. However, it was also known for its unpredictability and the tests it would impose upon those who sought its favor."

Arjun's eyes widened, captivated by the tale. He leaned in, his heart racing with anticipation, urging his teacher to continue.

"The Legend of Bhramapurta tells of a young prince named Ravi who embarked on a perilous journey to seek the river's blessings," Guru Rajan continued. "Ravi was known for his courage and his unwavering devotion to his kingdom.

He believed that the river held the key to prosperity and harmony for his people."

Arjun's imagination soared as he pictured the young prince venturing into the unknown, his resolve unwavering.

Guru Rajan continued, "Ravi faced numerous trials along the way—treacherous terrains, fierce beasts, and riddles that tested his intellect. Each obstacle was a test, an opportunity for him to prove his worthiness to Bhramapurta."

Arjun's mind raced, envisioning the prince's journey filled with challenges and moments of introspection.

"After days of arduous travel, Ravi finally arrived at the banks of the Bhramapurta," Guru Rajan said, his voice filled with reverence. "He stood in awe as the river's crystal-clear waters flowed gently, glistening in the sunlight. He offered prayers and poured his heart out, seeking the river's blessings for his kingdom."

Arjun's heart swelled with admiration for the prince's dedication and his desire to bring prosperity to his people.

"In that moment," Guru Rajan continued, "the river responded. Bhramapurta revealed its true nature—a reflection of Ravi's character and intentions. It rewarded him with wisdom, granting him insights and guidance to rule his kingdom with compassion and fairness."

Arjun sat in silence, absorbing the wisdom of the legend. He understood that Bhramapurta symbolized more than just a river—it represented the trials and tests of life, the pursuit of wisdom and inner growth.

Guru Rajan smiled at Arjun's thoughtful expression. "Remember, young one," he said, "the legend of Bhramapurta teaches us that the greatest blessings come not from external sources, but from the purity of our hearts, our unwavering dedication, and our willingness to face the challenges that come our way."

Arjun nodded, his heart filled with newfound understanding. The Legend of Bhramapurta had left an indelible mark, shaping his perspective on life's trials and the power that lies within.

As the night descended upon the village, Guru Rajan and Arjun sat in quiet contemplation, their spirits entwined with the ancient wisdom of the Legend of Bhramapurta—a tale that would continue to inspire generations to come.

Eclipse

In the bustling city of Mumbai, where skyscrapers reached for the heavens and the energy of millions vibrated through the streets, a tale of celestial wonder whispered through the air—a legend known as the Eclipse. It was a story that spoke of the rare and awe-inspiring event when the Sun and the Moon aligned, casting a spellbinding shadow upon the Earth.

In the year 2025, as the anticipation of a solar eclipse swept through the city, a young girl named Priya found herself captivated by the legend. Priya possessed a curious mind and an insatiable thirst for knowledge. She yearned to witness the magic of the eclipse, to witness the dance between light and shadow that would momentarily transform the city.

As the day of the eclipse drew near, Priya prepared herself. Armed with a pair of eclipse glasses and a heart filled with excitement, she ventured to an open terrace that offered an unobstructed view of the sky. Alongside her stood people of all ages and backgrounds, united in their eagerness to witness this celestial spectacle.

As the clock neared the appointed hour, a hush fell upon the city. The sky darkened, and a sense of anticipation hung in the air. Priya's pulse quickened, her gaze fixed upon the heavens.

And then, it happened—the Moon slowly began to slide across the face of the Sun, casting an eerie darkness upon the landscape. Priya slipped on her eclipse glasses, her eyes wide with wonder as she watched the celestial ballet unfold.

As the Moon covered more and more of the Sun, a sense of awe washed over the city. Streetlights flickered on, casting an ethereal glow upon the streets. The sounds of car horns and bustling activity gave way to a hushed reverence, as if the city itself held its breath.

Priya stood mesmerized, her heart pounding with each passing moment. She witnessed the world around her transform—shadows deepened, colors grew muted, and the atmosphere crackled with an otherworldly energy. Birds ceased their chirping, finding shelter amidst the trees, as if paying homage to the celestial spectacle.

Time seemed to stand still as the Moon continued its celestial journey, obscuring more of the Sun's radiant face. The city held its collective breath, engrossed in the grandeur of the moment.

And then, at the peak of the eclipse, when the Sun appeared as a mere sliver of light amidst a backdrop of darkness, a collective gasp escaped the lips of the onlookers. The city was bathed in an ethereal glow—the golden ring of the Sun's corona, a celestial crown that adorned the darkened sky.

Priya's heart swelled with emotion as she witnessed this rare cosmic spectacle. She understood the power of the eclipse—the reminder that even in the midst of darkness, there is beauty and light to be found. The legend of the eclipse became etched in her memory, a testament to the wonder and harmony that exists in the universe.

As the eclipse gradually receded, the city emerged from its temporary twilight. Sunlight once again bathed the streets, as if a hidden switch had been flipped, rekindling the city's vibrant energy.

Priya rejoiced, her spirit lifted by the experience. The legend of the eclipse had become a part of her, a tale she would share with future generations. It served as a reminder that amidst the hustle and bustle of city life, there are moments of cosmic beauty that connect us to the grandeur of the universe.

And so, as the people of Mumbai dispersed, returning to their daily lives, they carried with them the memory of the Eclipse—a testament to the power of nature, the allure of the unknown, and the magic that resides in the celestial dance between the Sun and the Moon.

Legend of the Lunar Eclipse

In the enchanting landscapes of Scandinavia, where snow-capped mountains pierced the sky and the Northern Lights danced across the horizon, a mystical legend whispered through the fjords—the Legend of the Lunar Eclipse. It was a tale that spoke of the moon's transformation into a celestial wonder, casting a spellbinding glow upon the land.

In a small village nestled by the coast, the villagers gathered around roaring fires, their faces illuminated by the flickering flames. Elders spoke in hushed tones, recounting the legend that had been passed down through countless generations.

According to the legend, in the depths of winter, when the full moon reached its zenith, it would be enveloped by the Earth's shadow—a phenomenon known as a lunar eclipse. During this celestial spectacle, the moon would don a mysterious hue, captivating all who beheld it.

In the year 1532, a young boy named Erik listened intently to the tale, his eyes wide with wonder. He yearned to witness the magic of the lunar eclipse for himself, to experience the ethereal transformation that occurred when the moon donned its celestial mask.

As the day of the lunar eclipse approached, Erik prepared himself. Wrapped in furs to protect against the biting cold, he ventured to a remote hilltop that offered an unobstructed view of the night sky. Alongside him stood villagers from far and wide, their hearts filled with anticipation.

As twilight gave way to darkness, a hush fell upon the land. The moon, full and radiant, began its celestial journey across the sky. Erik's breath hung in the frosty air as he observed the moon's majestic ascent, knowing that its transformation was imminent.

As the moon neared the center of the sky, a subtle shadow began to creep across its surface. The villagers gasped in awe as the moon's luminescent glow dimmed, giving way to a hauntingly beautiful shade a deep reddish hue, as if it had been kissed by the night itself.

Erik's heart quickened as he witnessed this celestial metamorphosis. The lunar eclipse cast a mystical aura upon the land, illuminating the snow-covered landscapes with an otherworldly radiance. It was as if the entire world held its breath, captivated by the enchantment in the sky.

As the lunar eclipse reached its peak, the villagers stood in awe. The moon, once a brilliant beacon, now glowed with an ethereal, otherworldly light. The sky seemed to vibrate with a mesmerizing energy, as if the universe itself had paused to witness this celestial spectacle.

Erik's eyes gleamed with wonder as he beheld the transformed moon. He understood the power of the lunar eclipse—the bridge it formed between the earthly and the cosmic realms. The legend became etched in his memory, a testament to the awe-inspiring forces that governed the heavens.

As the lunar eclipse gradually waned, the moon returned to its familiar radiance, casting its gentle light upon the world. The villagers, their hearts filled with a sense of wonder, exchanged knowing glances, forever united by the magic they had witnessed.

Erik returned to his village, his spirit uplifted by the experience. The legend of the lunar eclipse had become a part of him, a tale he would share with future generations. It served as a reminder that even in the darkest of nights, there is celestial beauty and harmony to be found.

And so, as the villagers dispersed, returning to their homes nestled in the Scandinavian landscape, they carried with them the memory of the Legend of the Lunar Eclipse.

A testament to the magnificence of the cosmos, the eternal dance between light and shadow, and the captivating allure of the moon in all its celestial splendor.

The Scribe of the Gods

In the majestic wilderness of Alaska, where glaciers carved their way through rugged mountains and the air was crisp with the scent of pine, a legendary figure emerged—the Scribe. It was said that the Scribe possessed a profound connection with the divine, tasked with transcribing the sacred teachings of God into words that would guide and inspire humanity.

In a small village nestled near the heart of Alaska's wilderness, the people gathered around a flickering fire, their faces illuminated by its warm glow. The elders spoke in reverent tones, recounting the legend that had been passed down through generations.

According to the legend, in the year 1700, a young woman named Elara discovered an ancient manuscript hidden within the depths of a sacred cave. As she held the delicate parchment in her hands, she felt a surge of divine energy course through her veins—a calling to fulfill a sacred duty.

Guided by an unseen force, Elara devoted her life to the task of becoming the Scribe. She immersed herself in the teachings of God, dedicating countless hours to transcribing and illuminating the sacred words. Her pen danced across the pages, capturing the wisdom and love that flowed from the divine source.

As word of Elara's profound connection spread, people from far and wide sought her guidance and sought to learn from the teachings she recorded. Her presence became a beacon of hope and enlightenment, drawing seekers from distant lands to the Alaskan wilderness.

In the year 1725, as Elara's role as the Scribe deepened, she established a secluded sanctuary within the heart of Alaska—a place where seekers could gather, learn, and embrace the divine teachings. The sanctuary, known as Haven's Reach, nestled amidst towering peaks and pristine lakes, became a sanctuary for those seeking spiritual nourishment.

Generations passed, and the legend of the Scribe continued to flourish within the sanctuary's hallowed halls. Each successor of Elara, chosen for their unwavering dedication and pure heart, inherited the sacred duty to transcribe the teachings of God, passing down the wisdom to future generations.

Within the walls of Haven's Reach, seekers from all walks of life found solace and inspiration. They studied the sacred texts, meditated in the tranquil gardens, and listened to the whispers of the divine winds. The teachings of the Scribe permeated their lives, guiding them toward love, compassion, and the pursuit of truth.

As the years unfolded, the sanctuary became a bastion of knowledge and spiritual growth, drawing seekers from across the globe to the heart of Alaska. Haven's Reach became a testament to the enduring power of the Scribe's sacred task—to illuminate the path of enlightenment and offer solace to those in search of divine wisdom.

And so, as the village and sanctuary continued to thrive, the legend of the Scribe lived on—a tale of a chosen individual in Alaska who, through the power of the divine connection, transcribed the teachings of God. Their words brought solace, enlightenment, and hope to all who embraced them.

In the pristine wilderness of Alaska, where the air was pure and the natural beauty awe-inspiring, the legend of the Scribe served as a reminder to humanity—of the profound connection between the divine and the human, and the eternal quest for spiritual enlightenment that lies within each individual's heart.

The Man in the Red Suit

In the bustling city of Casablanca, Morocco, a tale of mystery and intrigue whispered through the labyrinthine streets—a legend known as the Man in the Red Suit. It was said that in the year 1486, during the vibrant era of Moorish rule, a mysterious figure donning a vibrant red suit emerged, bringing both curiosity and trepidation to those who crossed his path.

In the heart of Casablanca's bustling marketplace, a young merchant named Ahmed prepared his wares for the day's trade. The air was heavy with the scent of spices and the lively chatter of the townsfolk. But beneath the bustling facade, a sense of anticipation simmered, for rumors of the enigmatic Man in the Red Suit had reached the city.

Ahmed had heard tales of this enigmatic figure—his flamboyant attire, his mysterious demeanor, and his uncanny ability to appear and disappear like a wisp of smoke. Some whispered that he was a jinn, others believed him to be a guardian of secrets, and a few even claimed he possessed the power to grant wishes.

One fateful morning, as Ahmed attended to a customer, a ripple of excitement coursed through the crowd. A man in a vibrant red suit emerged from the shadows, his presence commanding attention. His eyes gleamed with a mischievous sparkle, and an air of mystery enveloped him like a cloak.

Whispers erupted, spreading like wildfire, as the townsfolk huddled closer, their gazes fixed upon the enigmatic figure. Ahmed's curiosity piqued, and he cautiously approached, his heart pounding with anticipation.

The man in the red suit regarded Ahmed with a knowing smile, his voice carrying a hint of playful intrigue. "Greetings, young merchant," he said, his words laced with a musical quality. "I have traveled far to witness the splendor of Casablanca and the souls that dwell within."

Ahmed's pulse quickened. He felt a strange connection to this figure, as if their paths were destined to intersect. With a mix of curiosity and trepidation, he ventured forth, his voice trembling slightly. "Who are you, sir, and what brings you to our city?"

The man in the red suit chuckled softly, his eyes twinkling with mirth. "Ah, my dear Ahmed, names have little meaning in the realm of legends. Call me the Wanderer, if you must. As for my purpose, I am here to observe and perhaps lend a touch of enchantment to the lives of those I encounter."

Ahmed's mind swirled with questions, his curiosity ignited. "Are the tales true, then? Do you possess the power to grant wishes?"

The Wanderer smiled, his eyes seeming to hold the secrets of centuries. "Ahmed, the power to grant wishes lies not in the hands of others, but within the depths of one's own spirit. I merely serve as a catalyst, a reminder of the dreams and desires that reside within."

As the day unfolded, the Wanderer weaved through the vibrant streets of Casablanca, touching the lives of those he encountered. He shared stories that kindled hope, performed tricks that brought laughter, and inspired the people to embrace the magic that resided within their own hearts.

Through his interactions, Ahmed witnessed the transformative power of the Wanderer's presence. The people of Casablanca shed their burdens and embraced the joy and wonder that had long lain dormant within them.

And as the sun began its descent, casting a golden glow upon the city, the Wanderer bid farewell to the people of Casablanca. With a twinkle in his eye and a nod of his head, he disappeared into the labyrinthine streets, leaving behind a sense of enchantment and an indelible mark on the hearts of those he had touched.

As the legend of the Man in the Red Suit lived on, the people of Casablanca understood that magic and wonder exist not only in the tales of legends, but also in the everyday moments that make life extraordinary. They carried the memory of the Wanderer, forever inspired to embrace the enchantment that resided within their own souls.

And so, in the vibrant city of Casablanca, where the scent of spices mingled with the whispers of legends, the legacy of the Man in the Red Suit thrived—a testament to the power of enchantment, the beauty of human connection, and the eternal quest to embrace the magic that lies within us all.

Devil Dogs of Casablanca

Deep within the labyrinthine streets of Casablanca, where shadows twisted and secrets lingered, a haunting legend whispered through the city—a tale of terror known as the Spotted Devil Dogs. It was said that these malevolent creatures roamed the darkest corners of the city, striking fear into the hearts of those who dared to cross their path.

In the year 1922, as the moon hung low in the midnight sky, a young woman named Aisha found herself unwittingly entangled in the clutches of this chilling legend. Aisha had always been drawn to the macabre tales that circulated through the city, but she dismissed them as mere superstitions.

One fateful evening, as Aisha strolled through the dimly lit streets of Casablanca, an unsettling chill descended upon the air. The city seemed eerily quiet, its usual bustle replaced by a hushed silence. Aisha's instincts warned her of impending danger, but curiosity beckoned her deeper into the shadows.

As she ventured further into the heart of the city, a distant howl pierced the stillness, sending a shiver down her spine. Goosebumps prickled her skin, and she quickened her pace, hoping to escape the clutches of the encroaching terror.

But it was too late.

A pair of glowing eyes materialized from the darkness—a pair of eyes that mirrored the malevolence that haunted the legends. Aisha's heart pounded in her chest as she found herself face to face with the Spotted Devil Dogs.

The creatures, with their mottled fur and sharp fangs, lunged toward her, their snarls echoing through the night. Aisha screamed, her voice lost in the desolate streets, as she desperately sought an escape route.

With each step she took, the Spotted Devil Dogs pursued her, their predatory instinct sharp and unyielding. Aisha's breath came in ragged gasps, her heart pounding with fear as she weaved through the labyrinthine alleys, hoping to elude their relentless pursuit.

But the Spotted Devil Dogs were cunning. They anticipated her every move, their menacing growls growing louder, filling her ears with dread. Aisha's strength waned, her legs threatened to give way beneath her, and she knew that her fate hung in the balance.

In a last-ditch effort, Aisha darted into an abandoned building, hoping to find sanctuary within its dilapidated walls. The Spotted Devil Dogs circled outside, their snarls and scratching growing more frenzied. Aisha pressed herself against a wall, tears streaming down her face as she braced for their final assault.

But then, as if a miracle had intervened, the howls of the Spotted Devil Dogs were drowned out by a chorus of human voices. A group of brave locals, armed with torches and

  The Book of Legends

courage, had rallied to Aisha's aid, determined to drive away the malevolent creatures that haunted their city.

As the flames from the torches danced in the night, the Spotted Devil Dogs retreated, disappearing into the depths of the darkness from whence they came. Aisha's rescuers embraced her, their relief palpable, their eyes reflecting a shared understanding of the terror they had faced.

From that night forward, the legend of the Spotted Devil Dogs served as a haunting reminder of the shadows that lurked within Casablanca. The city's residents spoke of their encounter in hushed tones, forever wary of the darkness that prowled the streets.

And though the Spotted Devil Dogs retreated that night, their presence forever etched in the minds of those who witnessed their malevolence, the legend lived on—a testament to the enduring power of fear, the strength of community, and the eternal battle between light and darkness that unfolds within the shadows of the human soul.

Legend of the Weeping Statue

In the enchanting land of Norway, where fjords carved their way through majestic mountains and the Northern Lights danced across the night sky, a tale of mystery and wonder whispered through the ancient forests—a legend of the Weeping Statue.

In a small village nestled amidst the breathtaking landscapes, a young woman named Ingrid found herself drawn to the stories surrounding a peculiar statue that resided within the village church. The statue, carved from stone with delicate precision, depicted a figure of a sorrowful angel, tears forever frozen upon its serene face.

According to the legend, the Weeping Statue possessed the power to heal broken hearts and bring solace to those burdened by sorrow. It was said that when the moon shone its brightest upon the village, the statue would come to life, shedding tears of compassion and empathy.

Intrigued by the legend, Ingrid embarked on a quest to witness the mystical phenomenon herself. She spent her days exploring the village, gathering stories from the elders and immersing herself in the history and folklore that surrounded the Weeping Statue.

One moonlit night, as Ingrid stood before the statue in the dimly lit church, she whispered a heartfelt plea for solace, her voice echoing in the sacred space. She pleaded for guidance and strength to overcome the burdens that weighed upon her spirit.

As the moon reached its zenith, casting an ethereal glow upon the statue, Ingrid's heart skipped a beat. The stone figure stirred, and to her astonishment, tears welled up in its eyes, glistening like liquid pearls. She watched in awe as a single tear rolled down the statue's cheek, falling to the ground with a whisper.

In that moment, Ingrid felt a profound sense of peace wash over her. It was as if the statue's tears carried the weight of her sorrows, offering solace and understanding. She realized that the Weeping Statue was more than a legend—it was a symbol of compassion and a reminder that even in the depths of sorrow, there is solace and hope.

Word of Ingrid's encounter spread throughout the village, capturing the hearts and imaginations of the residents. They flocked to the church, seeking solace and healing from the Weeping Statue. They poured their hearts out, offering their burdens to the angelic figure with tear-filled eyes.

As the years passed, the legend of the Weeping Statue of Norway continued to flourish. The village became a sanctuary for those seeking solace, as people from far and wide ventured to witness the miraculous tears that brought comfort and renewal.

Ingrid, now an elder herself, stood alongside the statue in the church, her heart filled with gratitude for the solace it had brought her and countless others. She understood that the

Weeping Statue was a symbol of the resilience of the human spirit, a reminder that even in the face of sorrow, healing and hope could be found.

And so, within the ancient forests of Norway, where the whispers of the wind carried tales of mystery and the splendor of nature inspired awe, the legend of the Weeping Statue lived on—a testament to the power of empathy, the healing touch of compassion, and the eternal search for solace in the face of life's sorrows.

Lantern of the Black Forest

Deep within the depths of the mystical Black Forest, where towering trees intertwined their branches and an air of enchantment permeated the lush greenery, a tale of mystery and illumination whispered through the wilderness—a legend of the Lantern.

In a small village nestled on the edge of the forest, the villagers gathered around roaring fires, their faces illuminated by the dancing flames. The elders spoke in hushed tones, recounting the legend that had been passed down through generations.

According to the legend, deep within the heart of the Black Forest, a magical lantern resided. This lantern, said to be forged by ancient forces of light, possessed the power to guide lost souls, dispel darkness, and reveal hidden paths to those who sought its radiant glow.

In the year 1750, a young wanderer named Friedrich found himself drawn to the tales of the Lantern. He possessed an adventurous spirit and an insatiable thirst for discovery. Intrigued by the legends that surrounded the Black Forest, Friedrich set off on a journey to seek the fabled lantern.

As Friedrich ventured deeper into the forest's embrace, the air grew still and a sense of reverence settled upon him. The trees whispered secrets, their leaves rustling in anticipation of his arrival. His steps became deliberate, each footfall echoing through the wilderness.

Days turned into weeks as Friedrich navigated the labyrinthine trails, his heart beating with anticipation. He encountered mystical creatures and faced treacherous terrains, but his determination remained unyielding. He knew that the Lantern held the potential to illuminate not only the physical paths but also the depths of his own soul.

Finally, at the peak of his journey, Friedrich stumbled upon a hidden glade bathed in a soft, ethereal light. A stone pedestal stood at its center, upon which the fabled Lantern rested—a delicate, golden orb that glowed with an otherworldly luminescence.

Friedrich approached the Lantern with reverence, his palms trembling with a mixture of awe and trepidation. As he reached out, his fingers grazed the cool surface of the lantern, and a surge of energy coursed through his veins. The golden light enveloped him, illuminating the depths of his being.

In that moment, Friedrich understood the true power of the Lantern. It was not merely a physical source of light but a metaphor for the guiding force within each individual—the spark of inspiration, the courage to face the unknown, and the resilience to navigate life's darkest paths.

With the Lantern in hand, Friedrich emerged from the Black Forest, forever changed by his encounter. He shared his experience with the villagers, kindling hope and reminding them of the untapped potential that resided within their own hearts.

News of Friedrich's encounter with the Lantern spread like wildfire, attracting seekers from far and wide to the Black Forest. They ventured into the wilderness, their hearts open to the transformative power of the mythical lantern.

And within the depths of the mystical Black Forest, where towering trees whispered secrets and an air of enchantment prevailed, the legend of the Lantern lived on. It served as a beacon of inspiration, reminding all who ventured into the wilderness that even in the darkest of times, the light of hope and guidance could be found within themselves.

And so, as the villagers gathered around the fires, their faces illuminated by the dancing flames, they carried the legend of the Lantern in their hearts. They understood that amidst the wilderness, both external and internal, there existed a source of illumination—a metaphorical lantern that could light their way, dispel darkness, and guide them through the labyrinthine paths of life.

The Legend of the Lamp Wielder

In the ancient land of Almaria, nestled amidst rolling hills and shimmering rivers, a tale of mystical power and destiny unfolded—the Legend of the Lamp Wielder. It was said that in a time long ago, a chosen individual emerged, entrusted with a magical lamp that held the power to shape the course of their world.

In the year 1250, a young woman named Maya discovered an ornate lamp buried deep within the ruins of an ancient temple. As she brushed away the dust, a soft glow emanated from within, captivating her senses. Little did she know that her life was about to be forever transformed.

Word of Maya's discovery quickly spread throughout the land, reaching the ears of the wise elders who recognized the significance of the lamp. They revealed to her the ancient prophecy—the tale of the Lamp Wielder, destined to harness the lamp's extraordinary powers and bring balance to Almaria.

Embracing her destiny, Maya embarked on a quest to unravel the lamp's secrets and unlock its true potential. Guided by the whispers of the wind and the ancient texts, she traversed treacherous terrains, delved into forgotten crypts, and sought the counsel of sages who held fragments of knowledge.

With each step, Maya discovered new abilities bestowed upon her by the lamp. She could summon flames to illuminate the darkest nights, shape light into protective shields, and channel energy to heal wounds. The lamp became an extension of her being, a conduit for her power.

As Maya honed her skills, the land of Almaria began to change. The skies shimmered with vibrant colors, flora flourished in abundance, and creatures once on the brink of extinction returned to thrive. The people hailed Maya as their protector, their Lamp Wielder—a beacon of hope in a world beset by darkness.

Yet, Maya soon realized that her journey was not solely about mastering her powers. The lamp carried a weight of responsibility that extended beyond her personal ambitions. It was a tool of transformation, a symbol of unity, and a catalyst for change.

With newfound purpose, Maya rallied the people of Almaria. She encouraged them to embrace the light within themselves, to kindle the flames of compassion and understanding, and to protect the fragile balance of their world. Together, they stood as guardians, defenders of Almaria's harmony.

As the years passed, Maya's legend spread far and wide, transcending time and borders. The tale of the Lamp Wielder inspired generations to come, reminding them of the power that lay within their grasp—the power to illuminate, to heal, and to guide.

And so, in the mystical land of Almaria, where the light danced through ancient ruins and hope thrived amidst the shadows, the legend of the Lamp Wielder endured—a testament to the transformative power of destiny, the strength of unity, and the eternal light that resides within the hearts of all who dare to embrace it.

Tale of the Light Bringer

In the picturesque landscapes of present-day Norway, where mountains pierced the sky and fjords sparkled with pristine beauty, a legend whispered through the valleys—a tale of the Light Bringer. It was said that in times of darkness and despair, a chosen one would emerge to bring illumination and hope to the people.

In the year 2023, a young woman named Freya found herself drawn to the stories of the Light Bringer. She possessed a compassionate heart and a burning desire to make a difference in the world. Intrigued by the legends that echoed through the land, Freya embarked on a journey to uncover the truth and embrace her destiny.

As she traversed the breathtaking landscapes of Norway, Freya encountered elders and wise folk who spoke of an ancient prophecy. It foretold the coming of the Light Bringer—a person endowed with extraordinary abilities and an unwavering spirit to ignite the flame of hope in the hearts of humanity.

Guided by her intuition, Freya found herself in a remote village nestled amidst the fjords. The villagers welcomed her with open arms, sensing her connection to the legend. They shared tales of a sacred artifact—the Beacon of Lumina, a mystical object said to contain the essence of the Light Bringer's power.

Eager to fulfill her role as the Light Bringer, Freya delved deep into the legends and rituals that surrounded the Beacon of Lumina. She studied ancient texts, consulted with the village elders, and sought spiritual guidance from the land itself.

As Freya's knowledge grew, so too did her abilities. She discovered that she could harness the energy of light, casting luminous rays that dispelled darkness and inspired courage. Her presence alone seemed to ignite a spark within the hearts of those she encountered, filling them with a renewed sense of purpose and determination.

With the Beacon of Lumina in hand, Freya journeyed throughout the land, spreading her message of hope and empowerment. Wherever she went, people gathered, drawn to her radiant presence and the wisdom that flowed from her lips. She kindled the fire of compassion, urging individuals to embrace unity, and to seek common ground amidst their differences.

Word of Freya's extraordinary powers and her mission to illuminate the world spread like wildfire. The people hailed her as the embodiment of the Light Bringer—the catalyst for positive change and the guiding light in times of adversity.

As Freya traveled, she witnessed the transformation that unfolded in her wake. Communities rallied together, setting aside their differences to work towards a common vision. Acts of kindness and compassion blossomed, weaving a tapestry of unity and understanding throughout the land.

And so, in the present-day landscapes of Norway, where the majestic beauty of nature intertwined with the resilience of the human spirit, the legend of the Light Bringer lived on—a reminder that each individual possesses the power to ignite the flame of hope, to bring light to even the darkest corners, and to illuminate the path towards a brighter future.

As Freya continued her journey, her heart filled with gratitude. She understood that the legend of the Light Bringer was not just a story of myth and lore but a call to action for all who yearned to make a difference. Together, they would forge a path of light, inspiring the world to embrace compassion, unity, and the transformative power of hope.

A Tale of a Traveling Monk

In the ancient and serene landscapes of Japan, where cherry blossoms painted the spring and mist enveloped the mountains, a legend echoed through the villages—a tale of a Traveling Monk. It was said that this enigmatic figure wandered the countryside, offering wisdom and solace to those he encountered on his journey.

In the year 1600, during the Edo period, a young man named Takeshi set foot on the path of enlightenment. Inspired by the legends of the Traveling Monk, he embarked on a pilgrimage across the breathtaking landscapes of Japan, seeking wisdom and spiritual growth.

With a simple staff in hand and a humble robe adorning his frame, Takeshi ventured from village to village, temple to temple, immersing himself in the teachings of the ancient masters. He embraced the ascetic lifestyle, living off the kindness of strangers and finding solace in the beauty of nature that surrounded him.

Along his journey, Takeshi encountered people from all walks of life—farmers tending to their crops, artisans honing their craft, and nobles seeking inner peace. He listened to their stories, offering a compassionate ear and words of guidance that resonated with the essence of their souls.

The legend of the Traveling Monk spread like wildfire, carried on the winds of gratitude and awe. Villagers prepared simple meals and offered him shelter, eager to receive his blessings and wisdom. They marveled at his serene presence, sensing the deep well of knowledge and spiritual insight that emanated from within.

As Takeshi journeyed deeper into the heartland of Japan, he encountered challenges that tested his faith and commitment. Yet, he remained steadfast, drawing strength from the teachings and experiences that had shaped him along the way.

Takeshi's reputation as a wise and compassionate guide grew, drawing people from far and wide to seek his counsel. His gentle presence and profound insights touched the hearts of those who crossed his path, instilling a sense of peace and harmony within their lives.

Through his teachings, Takeshi emphasized the importance of balance—the delicate interplay between the physical and spiritual, the pursuit of inner harmony amidst the chaos of the external world. He taught the villagers to embrace the impermanence of life and to find beauty in the present moment.

As years turned into decades, Takeshi's journey took on a deeper meaning. The legend of the Traveling Monk had become intertwined with his own existence, as he became a symbol of enlightenment and compassion for generations to come.

And so, in the tranquil landscapes of Japan, where ancient temples stood as testaments to the enduring spirit, the legend of the Traveling Monk thrived. Takeshi's legacy lived

 The Book of Legends

on, carried forward by those who had been touched by his wisdom and kindness.

As he reached the twilight of his own journey, Takeshi found solace in the knowledge that he had fulfilled his purpose as the Traveling Monk. He had spread seeds of wisdom and love, inspiring countless individuals to embark on their own path of enlightenment.

With a heart full of gratitude, Takeshi embraced the final stages of his pilgrimage, carrying with him the memories of the villages, the teachings, and the lives he had touched. And as he faded into the mists of time, his spirit remained, forever guiding those who sought the wisdom of the Traveling Monk—reminding them to cultivate compassion, seek enlightenment, and find solace in the simplicity and beauty of life's journey.

Tale of the Threads that Bind

In the ancient city of Rome, where history seeped through every cobblestone street and grand monuments stood as testaments to the past, a legend whispered through the corridors of time—a tale of the Threads that Bind. It was said that invisible threads connected people's lives, weaving a tapestry of destiny and shaping their fates.

In the year 60 AD, during the height of the Roman Empire, a young woman named Livia discovered she possessed a rare gift. She could see the ethereal threads that intertwined and enveloped individuals, connecting them to one another in intricate patterns. It was as if the very essence of their lives was woven together by an unseen hand.

As Livia walked the bustling streets of Rome, her eyes were drawn to the shimmering threads that trailed behind each person. Some threads were vibrant and strong, signifying deep connections and intertwined destinies. Others were faint, barely visible, representing fleeting encounters or missed opportunities.

Intrigued by her newfound ability, Livia delved into the legends surrounding the Threads that Bind. She sought wisdom from the Oracle at Delphi, consulted with sages and scholars, and studied ancient texts in pursuit of understanding the true meaning and power of these mystical threads.

As her knowledge grew, Livia realized that she possessed the unique ability to manipulate the threads. With a delicate touch, she could influence the connections between individuals, altering the course of their destinies. It was a gift that carried immense responsibility and the potential for great impact.

Driven by a desire to bring harmony and unity to Rome, Livia dedicated herself to using her gift for the greater good. She sought out individuals whose threads were intertwined in conflict or strife and sought to mend the frayed connections that threatened their harmony.

Through her efforts, rival families found common ground, lovers reunited, and enemies became allies. Livia's touch acted as a catalyst, knitting together the delicate threads of fate, bringing about reconciliation and a renewed sense of purpose.

News of Livia's extraordinary gift spread throughout Rome like wildfire. The people hailed her as the Weaver, the one who could mend the tapestry of their lives and bring balance to the city. They sought her guidance, eagerly sharing their hopes and dreams, trusting in her ability to shape their destinies.

However, Livia soon learned that manipulating the Threads that Bind came with a price. The delicate balance of fate and free will hung in the balance, and the consequences of her actions weighed heavily on her soul.

As she grappled with the moral implications of her gift, Livia realized that true harmony could not be achieved through manipulation alone. She understood that the beauty of the Threads that Bind lay in their organic nature—the delicate dance of connections and choices that shaped the human experience.

With newfound wisdom, Livia vowed to use her gift judiciously, allowing the threads to flow naturally and honoring the individual choices and paths that each person must navigate. She became a guide rather than a puppeteer, offering counsel and support as individuals weaved their own destinies.

And so, in the ancient city of Rome, where the echoes of emperors and gladiators still resounded, the legend of the Threads that Bind lived on—a reminder that while connections and fate may intertwine, it is ultimately the choices we make that shape our lives.

Livia continued to navigate the labyrinthine streets of Rome, her eyes attuned to the unseen threads that connected people's lives. She offered her guidance and support, helping individuals find their own path amidst the intricate tapestry of existence.

As time marched forward, the legend of the Threads that Bind inspired generations to embrace their interconnectedness and honor the power of choice. And though the threads remained invisible to most, their presence could be felt in the very fabric of Rome—a testament to the enduring power of fate, free will, and the delicate balance that governs the human experience.

The Song of the Ancients

In the annals of history, where tales of lost civilizations and hidden treasures abound, there exists a legend of a song—one so powerful and mysterious that it is said to hold the key to unlocking the secrets of Atlantis. This legendary melody, known as "The Song of the Ancients," was said to have been lost in time, its whereabouts unknown to all who sought its hidden truths.

In the present day, a young archaeologist named Amelia dedicated her life to unraveling the mysteries of the past. Fascinated by the legend of Atlantis and drawn to the enigmatic Song of the Ancients, she embarked on a quest to uncover the ancient melody and, in doing so, unveil the location of the mythical city.

Her journey took her to libraries, ancient ruins, and remote corners of the globe, piecing together fragments of stories and deciphering cryptic symbols. Amidst her research, Amelia discovered whispers of a long-forgotten manuscript—an ancient codex said to contain the elusive song and the key to unlocking the secrets of Atlantis.

Driven by her insatiable curiosity, Amelia traced the path of the codex, venturing to remote islands and venturing into treacherous jungles. She followed the whispers of the ancients, guided by the belief that the Song of the Ancients held the power to reshape the understanding of human history.

As Amelia delved deeper into her quest, she encountered skeptics who dismissed the legend as mere fantasy. But her unwavering determination and the echoes of ancient voices in her heart propelled her forward, urging her to continue on her path.

In the depths of a forgotten temple, buried beneath layers of time, Amelia uncovered the codex—an exquisite parchment adorned with symbols and musical notations. With trembling hands, she delicately unfolded the manuscript, as if unwrapping the secrets of a lost world.

As the notes of the song came to life on the page, Amelia's heart raced with excitement. She deciphered the musical script, feeling the resonance of each melody in her very soul. It was as if the song carried the weight of centuries, a beacon of light leading her towards the hidden truths of Atlantis.

With the ancient melody in her possession, Amelia embarked on a perilous journey across vast oceans, guided by the clues embedded within the Song of the Ancients. She traversed treacherous waters and braved tempestuous storms, driven by the hope of unraveling the mystery that had captivated generations.

Finally, as the sun kissed the horizon, casting a golden glow upon the water, Amelia arrived at a secluded island—an ethereal paradise hidden from prying eyes. It was there, amidst the whispers of the waves, that she discovered the remnants of a once-great civilization—the ruins of Atlantis.

As Amelia explored the submerged city, her heart swelled with awe and wonder. She realized that the Song of the Ancients had led her to the very heart of the lost kingdom—a testament to the power of legends and the enduring mysteries of the past.

In that moment, Amelia understood that the true power of the Song of the Ancients lay not merely in its ability to unveil a physical location, but in the inspiration it stirred within the hearts of those who dared to dream. It represented the unending quest for knowledge, the relentless pursuit of truth, and the magic that resides within the realm of imagination.

Amelia returned from her journey, forever transformed by her encounter with the Song of the Ancients and the lost city of Atlantis. She shared her findings with the world, reigniting a sense of wonder and curiosity in the hearts of all who listened.

And so, the legend of the Song of the Ancients and the search for Atlantis lived on—a testament to the human spirit's unyielding pursuit of knowledge and the belief that within the melodies of the past lie the clues to unlock the mysteries of our future.

Phantom Sports Car

In the vast expanse of the open roads in Oklahoma, where the winds carried whispers of forgotten tales, there existed a legend of a Phantom Sports Car—a red and white beauty that raced through the night, forever chasing a victory that had long since slipped away.

On NH 55, a stretch of road shrouded in mystery, locals spoke of a spectral car that emerged from the depths of the darkness. Its engine roared with a haunting melody, echoing through the empty plains as it surged forward with relentless determination.

The legend told of a legendary race that took place decades ago, where the fastest drivers from far and wide gathered to compete on the very roads that now lay silent and deserted. It was a fierce competition, a test of skill and courage that would leave an indelible mark on those who participated.

Amidst the whirlwind of screeching tires and cheering crowds, one car stood out—a magnificent red and white sports car driven by a fearless racer named Jake. He was a legend in his own right, renowned for his extraordinary skill and unwavering spirit.

As the race reached its climax, Jake's car surged forward, leaving his competitors in awe of his speed and precision. But fate, as fickle as it can be, dealt a cruel blow. In the final lap,

Jake's car veered off the road, crashing into the unforgiving terrain.

The crash claimed Jake's life, abruptly ending a promising career and leaving behind a legacy of unfulfilled potential. Since that fateful night, whispers began to circulate—tales of a phantom car, driven by Jake's restless spirit, that continued to race on NH 55 long after the race had ended.

Locals reported sightings of the spectral sports car, its vibrant red and white hues illuminating the darkness. It sped through the night, its engine roaring, as if trying to rewrite history and claim the victory that had eluded Jake in life.

Witnesses described the phantom car's relentless pursuit, its tires gripping the pavement, leaving fiery streaks in its wake. The echoes of a forgotten race reverberated through time as the Phantom Sports Car blazed past startled onlookers, forever locked in a race that would never end.

Drivers passing through NH 55 recounted encounters with the spectral car—moments where it appeared in their rearview mirrors, briefly raced alongside them, and then vanished into the ether. Some felt a chill in the air as the phantom presence made its fleeting appearance, while others claimed to have heard Jake's laughter carried by the wind.

Though many dismissed the sightings as mere urban legends, a select few believed in the restless spirit that inhabited the Phantom Sports Car. They saw it as a reminder of the eternal pursuit of victory, the undying passion that continues to drive those who dare to dream.

And so, on the desolate roads of NH 55 in Oklahoma, where the memories of a forgotten race danced in the night air, the legend of the Phantom Sports Car lived on—a testament to the unyielding spirit of a racer determined to claim victory, even if it meant forever chasing an elusive dream on the empty highways of eternity.

Tale of Heat Storms

In the sweltering heat of the Brazilian summer, a legend whispered through the air—a tale of Heat Storms that ignited the skies and shook the very foundations of the land. It was said that in the year 2023, a phenomenon unlike any other swept across Brazil, bringing forth intense waves of heat and unleashing the fury of nature.

As temperatures soared to unprecedented levels, the people of Brazil sought refuge from the scorching sun. They whispered stories of heat storms that raged through the cities, transforming the landscape and leaving their mark upon the land.

In the city of Rio de Janeiro, nestled along the picturesque coastline, the legend took hold. It was said that when the sun reached its zenith, a fierce gust of wind would rise from the sea, carrying with it an inferno of heat. The sky darkened as billowing clouds formed, pulsating with energy and foreboding.

As the Heat Storms approached, the air crackled with electricity, and the atmosphere became charged with a potent energy. Thunder boomed overhead, shaking the ground, while lightning streaked across the sky, illuminating the city in an eerie glow.

The people sought shelter, their hearts pounding with both fear and awe. They watched in wonder as the storm swept through, its intensity unmatched, devouring everything in its path. Buildings trembled as if bowing to the fury of nature, and the streets became rivers of scorching heat.

Yet, amidst the chaos, tales of resilience emerged. Stories were whispered of individuals who stood tall in the face of the Heat Storms—brave souls who rallied their communities, providing solace and support to those in need. They became beacons of hope, guiding others through the tempestuous heat.

As the storms subsided, leaving a trail of scorched earth in their wake, the people of Brazil banded together to rebuild and find strength in unity. They understood that the Heat Storms were not merely a manifestation of nature's wrath but a reminder of their collective power to overcome adversity.

In the years that followed, the legend of the Heat Storms in Brazil took on a different meaning. It became a symbol of resilience, a testament to the human spirit's ability to endure and rebuild, even in the face of seemingly insurmountable challenges.

Communities adapted, implementing innovative cooling systems and embracing sustainable practices to combat the rising temperatures. They forged bonds of solidarity, sharing resources and knowledge to protect their homes and loved ones from the scorching heat.

And so, the legend of the Heat Storms lived on in Brazil—a reminder of the fragility and strength of the human spirit, the importance of unity in times of crisis, and the resilience of a nation that refused to be defeated by the flames of nature.

As the years passed, the Heat Storms gradually subsided, leaving behind a legacy etched into the memories of the people. Brazil rose from the ashes, stronger and more determined than ever to face the challenges that lay ahead.

And amidst the sweltering heat of the Brazilian summers, where the legend of the Heat Storms permeated the air, the people walked with heads held high, knowing that they had weathered the fury of nature and emerged resilient, united, and ready to embrace a future where they could thrive, regardless of the trials that lay ahead.

Odyssey Space Rocket

In the sprawling landscapes of Florida, where palm trees swayed in the warm coastal breeze and the sky stretched out in an endless azure canvas, a legend soared through the air—a tale of a legendary rocket on its grand journey to space.

In the year 2025, at the Kennedy Space Center, preparations were underway for the launch of the most ambitious mission yet—the culmination of years of scientific exploration and human ingenuity. The rocket, aptly named "Odyssey," stood tall on the launch pad, its sleek metallic body gleaming in the sunlight.

The Odyssey was not an ordinary rocket. It was a marvel of engineering and a testament to the relentless pursuit of knowledge and exploration. Inside its towering structure, a crew of courageous astronauts prepared themselves for a voyage that would push the boundaries of human achievement.

As the countdown commenced, the air buzzed with anticipation. Spectators gathered from far and wide, their eyes fixed on the rocket, their hearts filled with a sense of awe and wonder. The Odyssey represented not only a technological marvel but also the dreams and aspirations of a collective humanity.

With a thunderous roar, the engines ignited, and the rocket ascended, piercing through the Earth's atmosphere.

The ground trembled beneath the spectators' feet as they watched the fiery trail left in the Odyssey's wake. It was a sight that stirred the soul, a reminder of the boundless potential that lay within the human spirit.

As the rocket hurtled towards the heavens, a hush fell over the crowd. The only sound that echoed was the beating of their hearts, as if in unison with the pulsating engines. Each observer held their breath, their eyes fixed on the ascending spacecraft, knowing that the journey it embarked upon represented the pinnacle of human achievement.

Through the window of the Odyssey, the astronauts gazed upon the Earth, witnessing the vastness of the planet and the fragile beauty that it held. They marveled at the blue jewel that hung in the darkness, a testament to the wonder of their home and the interconnectedness of all living things.

As the Odyssey continued its ascent, it left behind the confines of the Earth's atmosphere, venturing into the vast expanse of space. The astronauts, weightless in their capsule, floated amidst a sea of stars, a realm of infinite possibilities.

Their mission was not merely to reach the outer realms of the cosmos but to deepen our understanding of the universe and our place within it. They conducted experiments, observed celestial phenomena, and peered into the depths of the unknown, pushing the boundaries of human knowledge.

News of the Odyssey's mission spread across the globe, capturing the imaginations of people from all walks of life.

They followed the progress of the astronauts with bated breath, united in their shared wonder and excitement for the possibilities that lay beyond the stars.

And so, as the legendary rocket sailed through the cosmos, its mission became a testament to the indomitable human spirit—the relentless pursuit of knowledge, the desire to explore the unknown, and the courage to dream beyond the confines of Earth.

As the Odyssey continued its voyage, weaving through the constellations and venturing into uncharted territories, it left behind a legacy etched into the fabric of human history. It inspired generations to look up at the night sky, to dream of what lies beyond, and to carry the flame of curiosity and exploration into the future.

And amidst the coastal landscapes of Florida, where the legend of the legendary rocket soared through the air, the people walked with their eyes turned skyward, their hearts filled with the eternal spirit of discovery, knowing that within them lay the potential to reach the stars and forge a future that surpassed even their wildest dreams.

Legend of a Small Book

In the sun-kissed landscapes of Florida, where the waves caressed the sandy shores and the air carried whispers of untold stories, a tale of mystery and intrigue emerged—the legend of a small book written by an author after their death, hidden away during a tumultuous purge.

In the year 1984, during a time of political upheaval, a renowned author named Sebastian Mason found himself entangled in a web of controversy. His powerful words had challenged the status quo and unsettled those in power, leading to his untimely demise. Yet, unbeknownst to the world, Sebastian had left behind a final creation—a small book that held the weight of his unspoken truths and suppressed ideas.

As the purge swept through the land, confiscating and eradicating any trace of dissident literature, Sebastian's small book went into hiding. It was tucked away within the pages of a forgotten library in a quaint coastal town of Florida, awaiting its chance to resurface and reveal the author's final message to the world.

Years passed, and the library changed hands, its secrets unknowingly guarded by generations of librarians who saw the book as nothing more than a forgotten relic. But fate has a way of guiding those who seek the truth, and it was in the year 2021 that a young librarian named Emily discovered the hidden tome.

Intrigued by the book's unassuming appearance, Emily delved into its pages and discovered the profound words that had been carefully penned by Sebastian Mason. The book carried an air of melancholy and urgency—a plea to challenge the oppressive regime that had silenced him.

As Emily read on, she became immersed in Sebastian's words. They stirred her soul, igniting a fire within her heart that demanded justice and change. She felt the weight of responsibility to honor the author's legacy and ensure that his message reached the world, even in the face of danger.

Emily embarked on a mission to protect the small book and bring its truths to light. With every turn of the page, she discovered hidden symbols and encrypted messages—a roadmap to unveil Sebastian's secrets. She reached out to trusted allies, forming a clandestine group dedicated to the preservation of knowledge and the liberation of suppressed voices.

Together, they ventured into the shadows of the regime, navigating the treacherous landscape of surveillance and oppression. They disseminated the book's contents through covert means, sharing Sebastian's words with those hungering for truth and seeking the courage to challenge the powers that be.

As the small book gained notoriety, the regime grew increasingly desperate to suppress its message. They unleashed their forces, raiding libraries and hunting down anyone associated with the clandestine group. Emily and her allies became fugitives, their lives threatened by the relentless pursuit of the regime.

But they remained resolute, driven by the belief that the small book held the power to spark a revolution of ideas. It became a beacon of hope, inspiring the people of Florida to rise against oppression, to question authority, and to reclaim their right to freedom of thought.

In the face of adversity, Emily and her allies persevered, their collective determination growing stronger with each passing day. Their actions set in motion a wave of resistance, an uprising that swept across the land, shaking the foundations of the regime and challenging the very fabric of their control.

And so, in the sun-drenched landscapes of Florida, where the legend of the small book emerged from the shadows, the people walked with newfound courage and an unwavering belief in the power of words. They carried Sebastian Mason's legacy in their hearts, knowing that even in the face of death, ideas can transcend time and spark a flame that will never be extinguished.

Pterodactyl

In the remote backwaters of Australia, where the lush wilderness whispered untold secrets and the ancient landscapes hid mysteries within their depths, a legend took flight—a tale of a pterodactyl seen in modern times, defying the boundaries of time and captivating the imaginations of all who encountered it.

In the present day, a group of adventurous explorers embarked on an expedition deep into the unexplored wilderness of Australia. Their journey led them to a hidden valley nestled amidst towering cliffs and dense foliage—a place untouched by the modern world.

As they ventured further into the valley, their eyes widened with wonder as they caught sight of a creature that defied everything they knew. A majestic pterodactyl soared through the sky, its wingspan casting a shadow over the explorers below.

Mesmerized by the sight before them, the explorers stood in awe, their hearts filled with a mixture of exhilaration and disbelief. The pterodactyl was thought to have been extinct for millions of years, a relic of the prehistoric past. Yet, here it was, gliding gracefully through the air, as if bridging the gap between eras.

The legend of the pterodactyl had long persisted among the locals, who spoke of a creature known as the "Ancient

Sky Guardian." It was said to possess immense wisdom and served as a symbol of the enduring spirit of the land.

As the explorers observed the majestic creature, they felt a profound connection to the ancient world—a bridge between the past and the present. The pterodactyl's presence seemed to echo the resilience and timelessness of Australia's wilderness, reminding them that the earth held secrets far greater than they could ever fathom.

Word of their extraordinary encounter spread, drawing scientists, researchers, and nature enthusiasts from around the world. They flocked to the backwaters of Australia, eager to witness the enigmatic pterodactyl and unlock the mysteries it held.

As the scientific community began to study the creature, theories emerged about its presence in the modern world. Some believed it to be a long-lost descendant of its prehistoric ancestors, adapting and surviving in the hidden corners of the Australian wilderness.

Others speculated that the pterodactyl's existence was a testament to the resilience of life itself—a reminder that the forces of evolution could transcend time, defying the constraints of what was once thought to be possible.

Amidst the excitement and wonder surrounding the pterodactyl, there emerged a deep reverence for the creature—an understanding that it represented not only a remarkable biological discovery but also a symbol of the delicate balance between the past, present, and future.

The pterodactyl's presence served as a catalyst for conservation efforts, inspiring a newfound appreciation for the wilderness and its inhabitants. People rallied together to protect the ancient landscapes of Australia, ensuring that future generations could witness the magic that unfolded within its borders.

And so, in the remote backwaters of Australia, where the legend of the pterodactyl took flight, the people walked with their eyes turned skyward, forever captivated by the mysteries that dwelled within the ancient wilderness. They carried the legend in their hearts, knowing that the bonds between the past and present were stronger than they could have ever imagined.

PART III

Guardians, Gods & Mythical Beasts

*

Ode to the Dreamers

In the rolling hills of Kentucky, where the melodies of nature danced on the breeze and the dreams of individuals took flight, an ode to the dreamers emerged—a swan song celebrating the audacity of those who dared to transform their dreams into reality.

In the small town of Willowbrook, nestled amidst picturesque landscapes and bustling with the charm of a tight-knit community, there lived a diverse array of dreamers. Among them was Amelia, a young artist with a heart filled with ambition and a canvas bursting with colors waiting to be unveiled.

Amelia's dreams reached far beyond the borders of Willowbrook. She longed to share her art with the world, to inspire others with the beauty she saw in the ordinary. With unwavering determination, she worked tirelessly, honing her craft and pouring her heart and soul into each stroke of her brush.

As her passion flourished, Amelia became a beacon of inspiration in her community. She encouraged others to pursue their own dreams, to embrace their talents and push beyond the boundaries of what was deemed possible. The small town became a gathering place for dreamers, a sanctuary where aspirations flourished and hope thrived.

Word of Willowbrook's dreamers began to spread, attracting individuals from far and wide who sought solace and guidance on their own creative journeys. They gathered in quaint cafes and vibrant art studios, sharing stories and collaborating on projects that reflected the depth of their collective imagination.

The dreamers of Willowbrook formed an interconnected web, supporting one another through triumphs and setbacks. They understood the hardships that accompanied the pursuit of dreams—the doubt, the uncertainty, and the fear of failure. But they also embraced the unyielding belief that dreams were the fuel that propelled individuals towards their truest selves.

As the years passed, the dreamers' endeavors transcended the boundaries of Willowbrook. The town became known as a hub of creativity and innovation, drawing visitors who sought to witness the magic that unfolded within its borders.

Amelia, now a seasoned artist, took it upon herself to organize an annual celebration—an ode to the dreamers that had transformed Willowbrook into a haven of possibility. The festival showcased art in all its forms, from visual masterpieces to musical symphonies, from the written word to the culinary arts. It was a testament to the power of dreams, a swan song that resounded throughout the town.

During the festival, the dreamers came together, their passions intermingling and igniting sparks of inspiration. Their creations adorned the streets, transforming

Willowbrook into a tapestry of imagination and wonder. Visitors marveled at the sheer audacity of the dreamers, their determination evident in every stroke of a brush, every note played, and every story shared.

In the twilight hours, as the festival reached its crescendo, Amelia took the stage. She shared her own journey, the highs and lows that had shaped her path. With passion in her voice and a glimmer in her eyes, she reminded everyone of the transformative power of dreams—the ability to defy odds, challenge conventions, and bring forth a reality more vibrant than any imagined.

And so, in the rolling hills of Kentucky, where the ode to the dreamers resounded, the people walked with heads held high, forever inspired by the collective courage and resilience of those who dared to chase their dreams. They carried the spirit of Willowbrook in their hearts, knowing that within their own aspirations lay the power to shape their destinies and create a world brimming with endless possibilities.

The Talking Whale

In the heartland of Oklahoma City, where the rhythm of life flowed with the heartbeat of the nation, a legend emerged—one that spoke of a talking whale, captivating the imagination of all who heard its tale.

In the summer of 1988, a group of children embarked on a wondrous adventure. They had heard whispers of a legendary creature—a whale that possessed the ability to communicate with humans. Driven by curiosity and a thirst for the extraordinary, they set out to uncover the truth behind the myth.

Their journey took them to a small lake nestled within the city, its serene waters reflecting the vibrant hues of the setting sun. It was there, beneath the shimmering surface, that the children caught a glimpse of a majestic creature—the talking whale.

With wide eyes and hearts brimming with excitement, they approached the water's edge. The whale surfaced, its glistening body cutting through the calm lake with grace. And then, to their amazement, it began to speak.

The whale's voice, melodic and deep, resonated through the air, carrying messages of wisdom and wonder. It shared tales of forgotten realms and untold adventures, captivating the children with its storytelling prowess.

News of the talking whale spread like wildfire, drawing crowds from near and far. People flocked to the lake, eager to witness the extraordinary creature and listen to its enchanting words. The city buzzed with anticipation, its spirit uplifted by the legend that had taken hold.

As the days turned into weeks, the talking whale became a symbol of hope and unity. Its words carried a message of harmony, encouraging people to listen to the voices of nature and each other. It spoke of the importance of preserving the environment and nurturing the bonds of compassion that connected all living beings.

But legends have a way of flickering like fleeting flames. As the seasons changed and the years passed, the talking whale gradually faded from the collective memory. Some dismissed it as a childhood fantasy, while others clung to the belief that the creature had returned to the depths of the ocean, carrying its wisdom and magic with it.

Yet, within the hearts of those who had witnessed the talking whale's presence, its legacy endured. It became a symbol of the extraordinary possibilities that lay hidden within the fabric of the everyday. It served as a reminder to embrace the wonders of the natural world and to listen with open hearts and minds to the voices that spoke from unexpected sources.

And so, in the heartland of Oklahoma City, where the legend of the talking whale once captivated the imagination, the people carried a spark of wonder, forever inspired by the notion that magic could be found in the most unexpected places. They walked with a renewed appreciation for the beauty of nature and the power of stories, knowing that the whispers of legends held the potential to shape their lives and connect them to something far greater than themselves.

A Tale of the Golden Tongue and its Enchanting Magic

In the vibrant landscapes of Peru, where the echoes of ancient civilizations whispered through the valleys and the spirit of mysticism hung in the air, a legend unfolded—a tale of the Golden Tongue and its enchanting magic.

High in the Andean mountains, nestled amidst mist-shrouded peaks, there lived a young girl named Amara. She possessed a gift bestowed upon her by the gods—a golden tongue that held the power to weave spells and bring forth extraordinary miracles.

Amara's legend spread far and wide, capturing the imaginations of those who sought the touch of magic in their lives. From distant villages to bustling cities, people flocked to witness her extraordinary ability, drawn to the hope and wonder that radiated from her being.

With every word Amara spoke, her golden tongue unleashed a symphony of enchantment. She brought barren fields to life, coaxing vibrant flowers to bloom in the harshest of landscapes. She healed the sick and mended broken hearts, her voice carrying the soothing balm of solace and restoration.

News of Amara's wondrous gift reached the ears of a powerful ruler, the Lord of the Sun, who resided in a palace adorned with gold and gemstones. The Lord of the Sun, consumed by jealousy and greed, sought to possess Amara's golden tongue, believing it would grant him unparalleled power and control.

Under the cover of night, the Lord of the Sun dispatched his most loyal guards to capture Amara and bring her to his palace. But the spirit of the mountains, aware of the looming threat, whispered a warning to the young girl. In the darkness, Amara fled, seeking refuge amidst the ancient ruins of Machu Picchu.

As the Lord of the Sun's soldiers scoured the mountains in pursuit, Amara found solace among the moss-covered stones and sacred temples. She listened to the wisdom of the ancient Inca spirits, who taught her to harness the true essence of her gift—a power that could not be seized or controlled by greed.

Embracing her destiny as the keeper of the Golden Tongue, Amara ventured forth from her hiding place. With each step, she sang a melodic incantation that resonated through the mountains, awakening dormant magic that lay dormant within the land.

As the Lord of the Sun's soldiers closed in on Amara, they were met with a spectacle that defied their understanding. The mountains trembled, and the earth quaked, unleashing torrents of light and energy. In a burst of golden radiance, Amara transformed into a magnificent condor, her wings stretching across the sky with awe-inspiring grace.

From the heavens, Amara's voice resounded, carrying the echoes of freedom and liberation. She unleashed a gust of wind, swirling through the soldiers' ranks, scattering them like leaves in a storm. The Lord of the Sun, witnessing the futility of his pursuit, fell to his knees, humbled by the power he had sought to possess.

And so, the legend of the Golden Tongue continued to echo through the mountains of Peru. Amara, now a guardian of ancient magic, soared through the skies, using her gift to bring harmony and healing to the people she encountered. Her golden tongue became a symbol of hope and the enduring power of kindness and compassion.

In the vibrant landscapes of Peru, where the legend of the Golden Tongue danced through the valleys, the people walked with a renewed sense of wonder. They carried the memory of Amara's enchantment in their hearts, forever inspired to embrace the magic that resided within their own words and to use it to create a world illuminated by love and harmony.

Water Dwellers

In the picturesque landscapes of Scotland, where mist-clad hills embraced serene lochs, a legend whispered through the tranquil waters—a tale of the Water Dwellers, ethereal beings said to reside in the depths of a mystical lake. It was the year 2055 when the legend resurfaced, captivating the imagination of a curious explorer named Ewan.

Ewan, an adventurer with a thirst for the unknown, embarked on a journey to uncover the truth behind the enigmatic Water Dwellers. Guided by tales passed down through generations, he set his sights on Lochan Mor, a secluded lake nestled amidst the rolling Scottish Highlands.

As Ewan delved into the depths of the folklore, he learned that the Water Dwellers were believed to possess a deep connection with the mystical energies of the land. They were said to be ethereal beings, part human and part spirit, who possessed the ability to traverse between the realms of land and water.

With his equipment in tow, Ewan arrived at Lochan Mor, drawn by its aura of mystery. As he gazed at the tranquil waters, he felt a magnetic pull—a calling to uncover the secrets hidden beneath the lake's shimmering surface.

With cautious steps, Ewan waded into the cool waters of Lochan Mor. As he swam deeper, his senses heightened, and the atmosphere seemed to shift around him. The sunlight filtered through the water, creating an otherworldly glow that danced upon the lake's floor.

It was then, amidst the dappled light, that Ewan caught a glimpse of movement—an elegant figure gracefully gliding through the water. The Water Dwellers had revealed themselves, their ethereal beauty captivating his senses. They possessed an otherworldly grace, their iridescent scales reflecting the colors of the surrounding environment.

As Ewan observed the Water Dwellers, he sensed a profound harmony between the land and the water. They moved with a fluidity that mirrored the ebb and flow of life itself, embodying the interconnectedness of all existence.

The Water Dwellers, sensing Ewan's genuine curiosity and respect, beckoned him closer. They shared stories of ancient wisdom, their voices resonating with the gentle melodies of the lake. They spoke of the delicate balance between humans and nature, urging Ewan to cherish and protect the Earth's precious resources.

In their company, Ewan experienced a profound transformation. He understood that the legends of the Water Dwellers were not mere myths but reflections of a deeper truth—a reminder of humanity's interconnectedness with the natural world and the responsibility to live in harmony with it.

As the encounter drew to a close, the Water Dwellers bid Ewan farewell, their graceful forms fading into the depths of Lochan Mor. Ewan emerged from the water, forever changed by his encounter with the mystical beings.

From that day forward, Ewan dedicated himself to preserving the delicate balance between humans and nature. He shared his experience with the world, inspiring others to reconnect with the Earth and honor the interconnectedness of all life.

The legend of the Water Dwellers lived on, carried through the ages by those who understood the importance of protecting the precious ecosystems that sustained us all. In the tranquil lochs of Scotland, where the legend of the Water Dwellers whispered through the waters, the people walked with a renewed appreciation for the mystical forces of nature, forever united in their commitment to safeguarding the wonders of the world.

Tale of King Paula

In the lush landscapes of Venezuela, where the sun kissed the earth and the rivers flowed with untamed beauty, a legend unfolded—a tale of King Paula, the once mighty and kind ruler known for his boundless capacity for love. It was the year 1482 when the legend of King Paula began to take hold, captivating the hearts of the people.

King Paula was a revered figure, known for his benevolence and wisdom. His kingdom thrived under his compassionate rule, and his subjects lived in harmony and prosperity. He possessed a heart that overflowed with love for his people, and they, in turn, adored him with unwavering loyalty.

The legend spoke of a time when King Paula's kingdom faced a great turmoil—a relentless drought that withered crops, depleted water sources, and left the land parched. As the people suffered, King Paula vowed to find a solution, driven by his love for his subjects.

Guided by his unwavering determination, King Paula embarked on a journey deep into the heart of the Venezuelan rainforest. He sought the counsel of the ancient spirits that resided within the land—the guardians of nature and the keepers of its secrets.

For days and nights, King Paula traversed dense jungles and treacherous terrains, until he arrived at a hidden waterfall nestled within a sacred grove. There, he communed with the spirits, pouring out his heart's deepest desires—the restoration of his kingdom's prosperity and the well-being of his people.

Touched by King Paula's love and selflessness, the spirits granted him a magical gift—a golden goblet that possessed the power to transform his love into life-giving water. They instructed him to pour his love into the goblet and offer it to the barren earth.

Filled with renewed hope, King Paula returned to his kingdom, the golden goblet clutched tightly in his hands. As he poured his love into the goblet, it shimmered with an ethereal light, and droplets of pure water cascaded from its rim. With every drop that touched the ground, life sprung forth—a testament to the power of love and its ability to nurture and sustain.

The rain returned to the land, quenching the thirst of the earth and rejuvenating the once desolate fields. The crops flourished, and the rivers overflowed with abundance. King Paula's kingdom thrived once more, bathed in the blessings of love and gratitude.

The legend of King Paula spread far and wide, capturing the hearts of neighboring kingdoms and distant lands. It became a symbol of compassion and the transformative power of love. People from all walks of life sought King Paula's counsel, eager to learn from his wisdom and to embrace his teachings of love and kindness.

King Paula's legacy endured, woven into the tapestry of Venezuelan history and the hearts of its people. His reign became known as the Golden Era, a time of unity and prosperity that was forever etched in the annals of time.

And so, in the lush landscapes of Venezuela, where the legend of King Paula whispered through the winds, the people walked with hearts filled with love and compassion, forever inspired by the once mighty and kind king who taught them the true meaning of leadership and the limitless potential of love.

King Solomon

In the misty highlands of Scotland, where ancient castles stood tall and the tales of legendary kings echoed through the ages, there emerged a tale of the legendary Tratiean King—King Solomon. It was the year 1483 when the legend of King Solomon graced the lands of Scotland, captivating the hearts and minds of all who heard his name.

King Solomon was renowned for his wisdom, his unmatched intellect, and his profound connection to the mystical realms. His reign was marked by fairness, justice, and a deep sense of responsibility towards his people. His subjects revered him for his keen insights and his ability to navigate the complexities of both the physical and spiritual worlds.

Legends spoke of a time when King Solomon faced a great dilemma—a conflict that threatened the unity of his kingdom and challenged the very foundations of his rule. It was during this tumultuous period that his wisdom shone brightest, guiding him towards a resolution that would change the course of history.

News of King Solomon's wisdom reached the far corners of the Scottish lands, drawing scholars, philosophers, and seekers of knowledge from distant lands. They sought his counsel, yearning to learn from his unparalleled understanding of the human condition and the mysteries of the universe.

In his grand palace nestled amidst the Scottish highlands, King Solomon held court, surrounded by his advisors and scholars. The halls echoed with spirited discussions, as minds from different disciplines converged to unlock the secrets that lay before them.

Among those who sought King Solomon's wisdom was a young philosopher named Alistair. Intrigued by the tales of the legendary king, Alistair traveled from distant lands to the Scottish highlands, eager to witness the brilliance of King Solomon firsthand.

Alistair approached the palace, awe-struck by its grandeur. As he entered, he was greeted by the hushed murmurs of scholars engrossed in deep contemplation. The air was thick with anticipation as King Solomon prepared to share his wisdom with those assembled.

Amidst the grandeur of the court, King Solomon's presence commanded attention. His eyes sparkled with ancient knowledge, his voice resonated with authority, and his words carried the weight of centuries of insight.

Alistair listened intently as King Solomon addressed the gathered scholars. He spoke of justice, compassion, and the pursuit of knowledge. He shared wisdom that transcended time, unlocking the secrets of the universe and the true nature of the human spirit.

In the presence of King Solomon, Alistair's mind expanded, his perspective forever altered by the depth of understanding and profound wisdom that flowed from the Tratiean King's lips. He was inspired to seek truth, to challenge conventions, and to contribute to the collective knowledge of humanity.

As the days turned into weeks, Alistair immersed himself in the intellectual atmosphere of the court. He engaged in debates, exchanged ideas with fellow scholars, and expanded his own understanding of the world. The teachings of King Solomon became the foundation upon which Alistair built his own legacy.

The legend of King Solomon, the Tratiean King of Scotland, spread far and wide. Scholars and philosophers journeyed from distant lands to learn from the wisdom that emanated from the Scottish highlands. King Solomon's reign became known as the Golden Age of Enlightenment, an era that forever altered the intellectual landscape of Scotland.

And so, in the misty highlands of Scotland, where the legend of King Solomon whispered through the ancient stones, the people walked with minds awakened, forever inspired by the Tratiean King who exemplified the power of wisdom, justice, and the pursuit of knowledge. They carried his teachings in their hearts, knowing that enlightenment was not merely the accumulation of facts but the transformation of the soul, and that the quest for truth was an eternal journey that spanned generations.

A Tale of the Tyrant King

In the rugged landscapes of Scotland, where mist clung to the ancient hills and the spirits of the land whispered through the glens, a tale of a tyrant king emerged—a ruler who not only questioned the gods but also challenged their might. It was a time of darkness and upheaval, where the land trembled under the weight of tyranny and defiance.

The king, known as Malcolm the Fearless, ascended to the throne with a thirst for power that knew no bounds. With each passing day, his arrogance grew, and he questioned the very existence and authority of the gods who were revered by his subjects.

Driven by his desire to assert dominance over both the mortal realm and the divine, Malcolm declared himself the ultimate authority and decreed that the gods' power was nothing but a figment of imagination. He prohibited the worship of any deity and sought to eradicate all signs of divine influence from the land.

But the gods, angered by Malcolm's audacity and his attempt to challenge their might, conspired to teach him a lesson. They gathered their forces and cast a spell upon him, cursing him with a mysterious ailment—a deep sleep that would last for a hundred years.

As the curse took hold, Malcolm's tyrannical rule collapsed, and Scotland rejoiced in the newfound freedom from oppression. The land slowly healed, as if rejuvenated by the absence of Malcolm's malevolence.

Years turned into decades, and the tyrant king's story faded into legend. The people of Scotland learned to cherish the gods once more, finding solace and guidance in their ancient traditions and beliefs. They honored the spirits of the land, understanding the importance of their connection to the divine.

It was in the year 2121, a century after the curse had been cast, that a young historian named Eilidh stumbled upon an ancient tome, buried deep within the ruins of an abandoned castle. The book contained the forgotten tale of Malcolm the Fearless and his defiance against the gods.

Intrigued by the legend, Eilidh embarked on a quest to unravel the mysteries that lay hidden within the ancient text. She traveled across the land, visiting sacred sites and seeking the guidance of wise elders. As she pieced together the fragments of the tale, Eilidh uncovered a path to the slumbering king's resting place—a hidden chamber deep within the mountains.

With trepidation and reverence, Eilidh entered the chamber, where time had stood still. There, she found Malcolm, his body preserved in an eternal slumber. Overwhelmed by the weight of history and the power of the gods, Eilidh pondered the choice before her—to awaken the tyrant king or leave him to his timeless sleep.

In a moment of clarity, Eilidh recognized that the true power lay not in the defiance of the gods but in the humility to acknowledge their might. She reached out and whispered a prayer, invoking the gods to restore balance and offer Malcolm a chance at redemption.

The gods, moved by Eilidh's plea and her understanding of the greater truths, answered her call. They granted Malcolm a second chance, awakening him from his slumber and imparting upon him the wisdom born of humility.

As Malcolm opened his eyes, he was no longer the tyrant king of old. He had been humbled by his encounter with the gods and had learned the value of compassion, justice, and the divine connection that existed between mortals and the higher powers.

United in purpose, Eilidh and Malcolm set out to rebuild Scotland, this time with fairness, compassion, and reverence for the gods at the forefront of their rule. The land flourished under their just governance, and peace and prosperity returned to the Scottish people.

And so, in the rugged landscapes of Scotland, where the legend of Malcolm the Fearless once echoed through the glens, the people walked with hearts humbled by the wisdom of the gods. They carried the story of redemption and the reminder that even the mightiest of rulers could be transformed through humility and a deep respect for the divine.

Set in Stone

In the historic town of Salem, where tales of witchcraft and enchantment lingered in the air, a young witch named Eliza discovered a power that defied the confines of time. Set in stone, her story unfolded amidst the cobblestone streets and the whispers of ancient spirits.

Eliza was a curious and adventurous soul, with an affinity for magic that surpassed her tender years. She yearned to explore the depths of her abilities and unravel the secrets of the mystical arts that had long fascinated her.

One fateful evening, as the moon hung low in the sky and the town slept beneath its silvery glow, Eliza ventured into the forbidden forest. Guided by an unseen force, she stumbled upon a hidden clearing, where a peculiar stone stood at its center.

Inscribed upon the stone were cryptic symbols, etched with the ancient language of witches long gone. Drawn by an irresistible pull, Eliza approached the stone and pressed her hand against its weathered surface.

As her palm made contact, a surge of energy coursed through her veins. The stone resonated with her magical essence, awakening a dormant power within her. Eliza gasped as she felt the surge of ancient knowledge flow into her being, expanding her understanding of the craft.

From that moment on, Eliza's life transformed. She delved into the study of spellcasting and potion brewing, honing her skills with fervor and dedication. Her reputation as a young witch with unparalleled potential spread through the town of Salem, captivating the attention of both curious onlookers and those who feared the unknown.

However, Eliza's newfound power brought forth challenges and responsibilities she hadn't anticipated. The townspeople, steeped in their history of witch trials and superstition, regarded her with suspicion and fear. They whispered behind closed doors, accusing her of practicing dark arts and bringing misfortune upon the town.

Undeterred by the doubts and prejudices that surrounded her, Eliza resolved to use her powers for good. She sought to break the cycle of fear and ignorance, to prove that magic could be a force for healing and unity.

With each act of kindness and every spell she cast, Eliza began to win over hearts. She aided the sick, cured ailments, and offered solace to those in need. The townspeople slowly recognized the purity of her intentions and the depth of her compassion.

As trust grew, Eliza embarked on a mission to bridge the gap between the worlds of magic and the mundane. She initiated open dialogues, inviting the townspeople to witness the wonders of her craft and understand that their fears were born from misunderstanding.

Through patience and perseverance, Eliza fostered a newfound harmony between witches and non-witches.

Together, they celebrated the beauty of magic and the potential for transformation it held.

And so, in the historic town of Salem, where the echoes of witch trials still lingered, the people walked with hearts open to the mysteries of the craft. Eliza's story became a symbol of resilience and the power of compassion to overcome fear. The town flourished, and its legacy changed from one of persecution to one of acceptance and unity.

Set in stone, Eliza's journey inspired generations to come, reminding them that the power of magic lies not in its darkness or its ability to manipulate, but in its capacity to heal, connect, and bring light to the world.

Singers in the Shadows

In the picturesque island of Santorini, where whitewashed buildings hugged the cliffs and the Aegean Sea painted the horizon in shades of blue, a haunting tale whispered through the cobbled streets—a tale of two legendary sisters known as the Singers in the Shadows. It was a story of extraordinary voices that evoked envy even from the gods, and their tragic transformation into hideous creatures destined to dwell in sorrow.

Long ago, in the vibrant town of Oia, lived the sisters Elysia and Callista. From a young age, their voices resonated with an otherworldly beauty, captivating all who heard them. Their melodic harmonies could make the waves dance and the stars weep with joy. It was said that their singing possessed the power to heal the wounded and mend broken hearts.

News of the sisters' extraordinary gift spread far and wide, reaching the ears of the gods atop Mount Olympus. Jealous of the mortals' ability to command such divine sounds, the gods conspired to take the sisters' voices for themselves.

Under the cover of night, as Elysia and Callista sang their hearts out by the seaside, a shimmering light descended from the heavens. In an instant, their voices were stolen, leaving them silenced and bewildered.

The gods, not content with their mischievous act, further cursed the sisters, transforming them into grotesque creatures, forever bound to the shadows. Their once ethereal beauty was replaced with gnarled limbs, pale skin, and eyes that glowed with sorrow.

Heartbroken and filled with despair, Elysia and Callista retreated to the darkest corners of Santorini, forever mourning the loss of their voices and the life they once knew. They became known as the Singers in the Shadows, their lamentations filling the air at night, mingling with the sound of crashing waves.

The people of Santorini, awed by the sisters' tragic fate, kept their distance, believing them to be cursed beings. They whispered tales of the Singers, their voices carrying a haunting melancholy that touched the soul.

However, there were a few brave souls who saw beyond the sisters' hideous exterior and recognized the beauty that still resided within. These compassionate individuals ventured into the shadows, offering kind words and gentle gestures, seeking to ease the sisters' eternal sorrow.

In time, Elysia and Callista began to open their hearts to these compassionate souls, allowing glimpses of their true selves to shine through. Although their voices were forever lost, their spirits found solace in the compassion of others.

As the years passed, the Singers in the Shadows became not only a symbol of tragedy but also of resilience and the power of empathy. Their presence served as a reminder to cherish the gifts bestowed upon mortals, to value the beauty of voice and song, and to treat others with kindness and understanding.

And so, in the enchanting island of Santorini, where the echoes of the Singers in the Shadows danced through the narrow alleys, the people walked with a heightened appreciation for the power of song and the importance of compassion. The sisters' legacy became a testament to the enduring strength of the human spirit, even in the face of unimaginable tragedy.

Liway

In the tropical paradise of the Philippines, where palm trees swayed under the warm sun and crystal-clear waters sparkled, there was a legend that spoke of the magical transformation of ice into water. This story, passed down through generations, told of a mystical encounter that occurred in the heart of the archipelago.

In a small village nestled amongst the lush greenery, there lived a young girl named Liway. She possessed a spirit of curiosity and a deep love for nature. One day, while exploring the dense forest near her village, she stumbled upon a hidden grove, where a shimmering blue crystal lay nestled amidst a bed of leaves.

Intrigued by the glistening object, Liway reached out and picked it up, feeling a jolt of coldness surge through her fingertips. To her astonishment, the crystal began to melt in her hands, transforming into a small droplet of water.

With wide eyes, Liway observed the miraculous transformation before her. She realized that the crystal she had found was ice—an element that possessed the power to change its form and become water.

Filled with wonder and curiosity, Liway embarked on a journey to learn more about this mysterious phenomenon. She sought the guidance of the village elders, who shared ancient stories of elemental magic and the interconnectedness of nature.

They explained that ice, born from the union of cold and moisture, held the essence of water within it. When touched by warmth, it returned to its original state—transforming from solid ice to flowing water. It was a delicate dance between the elements, a reminder of the ever-changing nature of the world.

Inspired by her newfound knowledge, Liway embarked on a quest to share this wondrous discovery with her village. She gathered the children near a babbling brook, where she demonstrated the transformation of ice into water. With a playful spirit, she showed them how ice melted under the warmth of their hands, teaching them the beauty of transformation and the importance of appreciating the changing seasons of life.

As Liway shared her knowledge, the villagers marveled at the magic unfolding before them. They realized that nature held countless mysteries waiting to be discovered and understood. The legend of ice turning into water became a symbol of the interconnectedness of all things—a reminder that change was a natural part of life and that beauty could be found in every transformation.

From that day forward, the village embraced the legend as a teaching, passing it down through generations. They recognized the significance of water—the life-giving force that sustained their crops, quenched their thirst, and nurtured the bountiful beauty of their surroundings.

And so, in the tropical paradise of the Philippines, where the legend of ice turning into water echoed through the palms and the gentle waves, the people walked with a deeper appreciation for the delicate dance of nature. They understood that just as ice melts to become water, life too was a journey of transformation, reminding them to embrace the ever-changing rhythm of the world and find beauty in every phase of existence.

Story of the Season of Change

In the pre-16th century, in what would later become known as New York, there existed a legendary clan called the Yorkers. They were a tribe deeply connected to the natural world, attuned to the rhythms of the land and the ever-changing seasons that guided their lives. Among the Yorkers, there was a tale passed down through generations—a story of the Season of Change.

According to the legend, the Season of Change marked a sacred time when the land underwent a remarkable transformation. It was a period of transition between the vibrant hues of autumn and the stark stillness of winter, when nature revealed its most breathtaking spectacle.

As the air turned crisp and the leaves burst into fiery shades of red, orange, and gold, the Yorkers awaited the arrival of the Season of Change with anticipation. It was during this time that the spirits of the land were said to be most present, guiding their people through the shifting tides of nature.

The Yorker clan believed that the Season of Change held the power to bring about personal growth and renewal. It was a time when individuals were encouraged to reflect upon their journey, shedding old beliefs and habits to make way for new beginnings. They saw the changing landscape as a reflection of their own internal landscapes, reminding them of the impermanence of life and the constant need for adaptation.

During the Season of Change, the Yorkers gathered around a sacred bonfire, its flames dancing in harmony with the vibrant foliage that surrounded them. The elders would share stories of their ancestors, recounting tales of resilience and the strength found in embracing the ever-shifting world.

Among the Yorkers, there was a young woman named Maya, whose spirit burned with curiosity and a thirst for knowledge. She longed to discover the deeper meanings hidden within the Season of Change and how it connected to her own path in life.

Guided by her intuition, Maya embarked on a solitary journey into the heart of the wilderness. She ventured deep into the dense forests, her steps guided by the whispers of the wind and the rustling of leaves under her feet.

As she traversed the land, Maya encountered various symbols—a fallen leaf, a cascading waterfall, and the resolute gaze of an owl perched on a branch. Each encounter held a message, reminding her to embrace the ebb and flow of life, to find beauty in impermanence, and to trust in her own resilience.

Upon her return to the Yorker village, Maya shared her revelations with the tribe. She spoke of the wisdom she had gleaned from the natural world, emphasizing the importance of embracing change and finding strength in the midst of uncertainty.

Inspired by Maya's journey, the Yorkers began to view the Season of Change not merely as a transition between seasons but as a profound opportunity for personal and collective growth. They recognized that change was not to be feared but embraced, for it was through change that they could adapt, learn, and thrive.

And so, in the pre-16th century land that would become New York, the Yorker clan walked with a deep reverence for the Season of Change. They celebrated the cycles of nature, embracing the teachings of impermanence and resilience, knowing that within the changing tides of life lay the seeds of transformation and the potential for endless renewal.

The Story of the Mystical Cauldron

In the enchanting landscapes of Yorkshire, where rolling hills and picturesque villages dotted the countryside, there stood a legendary club known as the Mystical Cauldron. It was said to be a haven for those with magical inclinations, a place where the magically attuned people and creatures could gather and find solace in their shared gifts. The story of the Mystical Cauldron spanned centuries, intertwining the realms of the past and the present.

In the year 1344, during the medieval era, the Mystical Cauldron was a hidden gem tucked away in the heart of Yorkshire. The club's existence was known only to those who possessed magical abilities, their presence carefully concealed from the prying eyes of the outside world.

Inside the club, adorned with tapestries depicting mythical creatures and shelves lined with ancient spell books, members from all walks of magical life gathered. Witches, wizards, fairies, and other enchanted beings convened to share knowledge, exchange stories, and seek camaraderie in a world that often misunderstood their powers.

It was during this time that a young witch named Evangeline discovered the existence of the Mystical Cauldron. She had grown up in a small village, keeping her magical abilities hidden for fear of persecution. The discovery of the club offered her a glimmer of hope—a place where she could finally embrace her true self.

As Evangeline entered the club for the first time, she was enveloped in an atmosphere crackling with energy. The air buzzed with whispered incantations and the soft fluttering of wings. She was welcomed by a diverse array of magical beings, each with their own unique talents and stories.

In the heart of the Mystical Cauldron, there stood a grand cauldron—an emblem of unity and the club's mystical power. It was said that the cauldron had been imbued with ancient magic, acting as a conduit for the collective energies of the members.

Over the centuries, the Mystical Cauldron continued to thrive, attracting individuals from far and wide who sought refuge and belonging. The club's influence extended beyond Yorkshire, reaching magical communities across the realm.

In present-day Yorkshire, the Mystical Cauldron still stood, having withstood the test of time. Its secrets were no longer hidden, as the world had become more accepting of magic and its practitioners. The club now welcomed not only humans but also supernatural beings who had long inhabited the realm of folklore.

Among the members of the modern-day Mystical Cauldron was a young warlock named Oliver. He was born with an affinity for elemental magic, wielding powers over fire and earth. Oliver's journey led him to the club, where he discovered a sanctuary filled with kindred spirits.

As Oliver delved deeper into the world of magic, he uncovered the rich history of the Mystical Cauldron, connecting the threads of the past to the present. He learned of the legendary witches, wizards, and magical creatures who had come before him, leaving their mark on the club's tapestry.

With each gathering, the power of the Mystical Cauldron grew, its members bound by a shared purpose—to protect the balance between the magical and non-magical worlds, and to celebrate the beauty and wonder of their gifts.

And so, in the captivating landscapes of Yorkshire, where the legend of the Mystical Cauldron whispered through the winds, the magically attuned beings walked with a sense of belonging and community. They embraced their powers, finding solace and strength in the shared heritage of the club, forever united by the bonds of magic and the spirit of Yorkshire's enchanting realms.

The Enchanted Meadows

Deep in the heart of a mystical land, there existed a place shrouded in whispers and secrets—the Enchanted Meadows. Legend had it that within these meadows, wishes had the power to manifest into reality. However, those who dared to make a wish also had to bear the weight of a price, for every desire fulfilled demanded a sacrifice in return.

It was said that the Enchanted Meadows were accessible only to those with the purest of intentions and the bravest of hearts. Many had ventured into its depths, lured by the promise of having their deepest desires granted. But few had returned unchanged, for the meadows had a way of revealing one's true nature and testing the strength of their convictions.

In a small village nearby, there lived a young woman named Lila. She had heard tales of the Enchanted Meadows from her grandmother, who spoke of its magic with a mixture of fascination and caution. Despite the warnings of the price to be paid, Lila's heart burned with an unyielding longing for her wish to come true.

Driven by her yearning, Lila embarked on a journey through dense forests and treacherous terrain, guided only by the whispers of ancient tales and her unwavering determination. After days of traversing unfamiliar lands, she finally stood at the edge of the Enchanted Meadows—a place of ethereal beauty, where flowers bloomed in hues unseen and the air crackled with enchantment.

Lila cautiously stepped into the meadows, her heart pounding with anticipation. She walked among the vibrant flora, each step carrying the weight of her wish. As she reached a clear, open space bathed in golden light, she closed her eyes and whispered her deepest desire into the air.

A hush fell over the meadows, and a voice, gentle yet haunting, echoed through the air. It spoke of the price to be paid—the sacrifice required to turn dreams into reality. Lila's heart wavered, but her determination remained unwavering. She knew that sometimes, the greatest wishes demanded the greatest sacrifices.

With a resolute nod, Lila accepted the terms, knowing that her journey would not be without consequences. The meadows shimmered with a new intensity as her wish was granted, and her heart swelled with joy and gratitude. But even as her dreams came to fruition, a part of her knew that she would carry the weight of her sacrifice for the rest of her days.

As Lila left the Enchanted Meadows, she felt a profound change within her. The fulfillment of her wish had come at a cost, and she embraced the newfound wisdom that came with it. She returned to her village, forever changed by her encounter with the meadows.

In the years that followed, Lila's life blossomed with the fruits of her wish. But she never forgot the price she had paid, nor the lessons learned in the Enchanted Meadows. She carried within her a deep appreciation for the delicate balance between desire and sacrifice, understanding that every choice held consequences.

Word of Lila's journey spread throughout the land, and others were both inspired and cautioned by her tale. The legend of the Enchanted Meadows endured, reminding all who heard it of the complexities of wishes and the importance of considering the true cost of their desires.

And so, in the mystical realm of the Enchanted Meadows, where wishes did come true, the air whispered with cautionary tales and the echoes of those who had paid their dues. It served as a reminder that in the pursuit of dreams, one must tread carefully, for every wish granted demanded a sacrifice, and the true measure of one's character lay in how they faced the consequences of their desires.

Legends of the Mind & Spirit

***

Time Traveler's Ball

In the realm of infinite possibilities and the mysteries of the cosmos, a legendary event was held—a grand gathering known as the Time Traveler's Ball. The ball, orchestrated by the late Stephen Hawking himself, was a celebration of the wondrous concept of time travel, bringing together beings from different eras and realms to revel in the magic of traversing through time.

The venue was a stately mansion nestled amidst rolling hills, its grandeur transcending any specific time period. Stephen Hawking, known for his brilliance in the realm of theoretical physics, had left behind instructions for the ball to be organized and held in his honor following his passing, as a testament to his fascination with the possibilities of time.

As the sun dipped below the horizon, casting a blanket of darkness over the land, the doors of the mansion swung open, revealing a scene that defied conventional logic. Peculiar beings and individuals clad in garments from various epochs filed into the grand hall, their eyes gleaming with excitement and curiosity.

The Time Traveler's Ball transcended the confines of time and space, allowing for interactions that would be deemed impossible in the linear flow of history. Dinosaurs mingled with astronauts, Victorian ladies twirled with cyborgs, and ancient pharaohs engaged in conversation with futuristic beings. It was a sight that defied imagination and thrilled the senses.

In the midst of the festivities, the spirit of Stephen Hawking seemed to permeate the air, his voice resonating through the ballroom. He spoke of the boundless potential of time travel, urging those present to explore the mysteries of the universe and challenge the limits of their own understanding.

Throughout the night, conversations filled with wisdom and wonder echoed through the halls. Time travelers shared their experiences, their journeys spanning centuries and dimensions. They spoke of the complexities of altering the course of history, the delicate balance between cause and effect, and the profound responsibility that came with the power to manipulate time.

As the night wore on, a sense of unity prevailed—a shared understanding among the time travelers that they were connected by their love for the enigma of time. They reveled in the beauty of their differences and the shared thrill of experiencing the ebb and flow of history.

As dawn broke and the final moments of the ball approached, the time travelers bid farewell to one another, their hearts filled with newfound friendships and a deeper appreciation for the vastness of existence. They understood that, while time could be manipulated, the bonds they had forged transcended the constraints of temporal boundaries.

With the first rays of sunlight, the mansion faded into the mists of time, leaving behind only memories and a profound sense of gratitude for the extraordinary gathering that had taken place. The Time Traveler's Ball had served as a reminder that the exploration of time, while full of wonder and excitement, required the utmost respect and responsibility.

And so, in the annals of history and beyond the reaches of time itself, the legend of the Time Traveler's Ball lived on—a testament to the power of human curiosity, the boundless nature of the cosmos, and the enduring legacy of Stephen Hawking's quest for knowledge.

The Legend of York

In the bustling streets of New York City, amid the clattering of carriages and the hum of activity, there lived a legend known as The Legend of York. It was a tale that had woven itself into the fabric of the city, capturing the imagination of its inhabitants and forever leaving a mark on its history. Set in the year 1877, it told the story of a young girl named Amelia and her extraordinary journey through the labyrinthine streets of New York.

Amelia was a spirited and curious girl with a penchant for exploration. Her heart yearned to unravel the mysteries that lay hidden within the city's cobblestone pathways. She had heard whispers of a secret that could be unlocked only by those who possessed the courage to venture beyond the well-trodden paths.

One fateful day, as Amelia walked along the waterfront, her eyes were drawn to a peculiar map wedged between the pages of an old book in a dusty bookstore window. The map appeared to reveal a hidden route through the heart of the city—an enigmatic path that promised untold wonders and secrets waiting to be discovered.

Driven by a sense of adventure, Amelia purchased the map and set forth on her journey, embarking on a quest that would forever change her perception of New York City. Following the intricate markings and cryptic symbols, she wound her way through the labyrinthine streets, guided by an invisible hand.

As Amelia delved deeper into the heart of the city, the landscape transformed before her eyes. Gleaming towers and bustling thoroughfares gave way to cobblestone alleys and gas-lit streets reminiscent of a bygone era. The sounds of carriages and conversations faded, replaced by a mysterious silence that enveloped her every step.

With each turn, Amelia discovered hidden pockets of New York's rich history—forgotten landmarks and untold stories that had been buried beneath the passage of time. She uncovered the struggles and triumphs of immigrants seeking new beginnings, the vibrancy of street markets where voices mingled in a symphony of languages, and the resilience of a city perpetually in motion.

Amidst her explorations, Amelia encountered a group of like-minded individuals who shared her desire to uncover the city's hidden treasures. They formed an unlikely alliance, united by their love for New York and their quest for the truth behind The Legend of York.

Together, they deciphered the map's secrets, following its intricate pathways and overcoming numerous challenges. The map led them to forgotten neighborhoods, abandoned buildings, and secret chambers concealed within the city's fabric.

As Amelia and her newfound companions unraveled the mysteries of The Legend of York, they discovered that it was more than just a tale—it was a metaphor for the spirit of New

York itself. It embodied the relentless pursuit of dreams, the resilience in the face of adversity, and the unwavering belief in the power of the human spirit.

With their journey nearing its end, Amelia and her companions reached the final destination—the heart of the city. There, in a hidden sanctuary, they found a book, filled with stories of everyday heroes and extraordinary feats, forever etched in the city's history.

As Amelia closed the book, a profound sense of belonging washed over her. The legend had brought her closer to New York and its people, connecting her to the stories that had shaped the city's identity.

From that day forward, Amelia carried the spirit of The Legend of York within her, a guardian of the city's legacy and a keeper of its untold tales. She understood that New York's essence lay not only in its iconic landmarks but also in the intangible stories woven through its streets.

And so, in the bustling metropolis of New York City, where the echoes of The Legend of York whispered through the urban canyons, the people walked with a deeper appreciation for their city's rich history and the power of stories to connect and inspire.

 The Book of Legends

The Legend of the Yorkshire Beasts

In the rolling hills and picturesque landscapes of Yorkshire, a tale was whispered through generations—a legend known as "The Legend of the Yorkshire Beasts." It was said that deep within the heart of the region, mysterious creatures roamed the land, embodying the wild beauty and untamed spirit of Yorkshire itself.

According to the legend, these legendary beasts possessed a connection to the ancient forces that shaped the land. They were guardians of the Yorkshire moors, protectors of its rich history and untamed wilderness. Each creature represented a different aspect of the region's spirit, bound together by their shared love for the land they called home.

The first of these majestic beasts was the Yorkshire Lion—a symbol of strength and resilience. With a golden mane that glowed under the sun, the lion roamed the hills and valleys, its powerful roar echoing through the moors, reminding all who heard it of the indomitable spirit of Yorkshire.

The second creature was the Yorkshire Falcon—a creature of the skies, representing freedom and grace. With wings that stretched wide, it soared above the rugged cliffs and swooped down, its keen eyes surveying the vast landscapes below. The falcon reminded the people of Yorkshire to embrace their own aspirations and soar to new heights.

The third and final creature was the Yorkshire Stag—a majestic figure with antlers that reached toward the heavens. It embodied elegance and wisdom, leading the way through the ancient forests and guiding lost souls back to the path of discovery. The stag reminded the people of Yorkshire to honor the past and carry its wisdom into the future.

The legend spoke of a time when the Yorkshire Beasts would come together, their presence invoking a sense of awe and wonder in those fortunate enough to witness their unity. It was said that during the rarest of celestial events, when the moon kissed the sun and the stars aligned just so, the Yorkshire Beasts would gather at a sacred grove, where their collective power would illuminate the night and ignite the spirits of all who beheld their majesty.

For centuries, the people of Yorkshire held the legend close to their hearts, cherishing the bond between the land and its mythical guardians. They saw the Yorkshire Beasts as a reminder of their own connection to the untamed spirit of the region, inspiring them to face life's challenges with courage, to embrace the freedom of the open skies, and to cherish the wisdom gained from their ancestors.

And so, in the breathtaking landscapes of Yorkshire, where the whispers of the Yorkshire Beasts mingled with the wind, the people walked with a deep reverence for the land and a sense of awe for the legendary creatures that roamed its expanse. They honored the spirit of the Yorkshire Beasts and embraced the wild beauty that surrounded them, forever entwined in the tapestry of the Yorkshire legend.

Raj and His Time Machine

In the wake of the failed Time Traveler's Ball, held in honor of the late Stephen Hawking, the world moved on, dismissing the event as nothing more than an ambitious dream. But there was one person who refused to let go of the possibility—a young man named Raj.

Raj had long been captivated by the brilliance of Stephen Hawking and his exploration of the mysteries of time and space. Inspired by Hawking's legacy, Raj devoted himself to the study of physics, dreaming of uncovering the secrets of the universe.

Undeterred by the disappointment of the past, Raj worked tirelessly in his small workshop, driven by an unwavering determination to bring the Time Traveler's Ball to life. He poured over Hawkins's writings and theories, delving into the complexities of temporal mechanics.

After years of painstaking effort, Raj completed his invention—a functioning time machine. Filled with hope and excitement, he set the coordinates for the time and place of the ill-fated ball, determined to make the event a success.

With a flash of light, Raj materialized at the ball, greeted by a scene that seemed frozen in time. There, among the flickering candles and the decorations that had long lost their luster, stood Stephen Hawking himself, alive and well.

Raj's heart skipped a beat as he approached Hawking, his voice trembling with awe and admiration. He explained his purpose, recounting his journey through time to ensure that the event would not be forgotten, that its potential would be realized.

Stephen Hawking, his eyes twinkling with a mix of surprise and delight, listened intently to Raj's story. He marveled at the young man's tenacity and unwavering belief in the power of dreams.

In that moment, the Time Traveler's Ball was no longer a failed event of the past. It became a profound testament to the human spirit—the determination to push the boundaries of possibility and make the seemingly impossible a reality.

With Raj's arrival, the ball came alive once more. Time travelers from various eras materialized, their presence a testament to the power of Raj's invention and the enduring legacy of Stephen Hawking's ideas.

As the night unfolded, conversations filled the air, spanning centuries and dimensions. Time travelers shared their tales, exchanging knowledge and experiences that transcended the boundaries of time itself.

Stephen Hawking, surrounded by a multitude of vibrant characters from different eras, beamed with joy. He spoke of the endless potential of humanity, the beauty of curiosity, and the importance of embracing the unknown.

In that fleeting moment, Raj and Stephen Hawking stood side by side, united in their passion for unraveling the mysteries of time. The Time Traveler's Ball became a testament to their shared dream—a celebration of the human spirit's relentless pursuit of knowledge and exploration.

As the night came to an end, Raj bid farewell to the time travelers, their gratitude and admiration etched upon their faces. With a final nod of appreciation, Raj stepped back into his time machine, knowing that he had fulfilled his purpose—to ensure that the legacy of the Time Traveler's Ball would endure.

And so, in the annals of history and the realm of possibility, the legend of the Time Traveler's Ball lived on—a story of determination, inspiration, and the belief that even in the face of adversity, dreams could be realized. Raj's act of daring and his encounter with Stephen Hawking became a symbol of the extraordinary lengths to which the human spirit would go in pursuit of its greatest aspirations.

Skin Walkers

Deep in the mountains of Sacramento County, nestled within a secluded hiking trail, a legend whispered through the winds—a legend of the skin walkers. These enigmatic creatures possessed the ability to take the form of humans and mimic the cries of those in distress, luring unsuspecting travelers into their clutches.

As the sun began its descent, casting a warm glow upon the rugged terrain, the skin walkers emerged from the depths of the forest. They roamed the trails, their eyes glowing with an otherworldly light, and their footsteps as silent as the whisper of the wind.

Hikers who ventured along the trail during the twilight hours would occasionally encounter the skin walkers, mistaking them for fellow adventurers in need. The creatures had a cunning ability to mimic the cries for help, their voices echoing through the trees with a haunting authenticity.

One such evening, a group of friends set out on an adventure, unaware of the lurking danger that awaited them. Amy, Jack, and Sarah were avid hikers, drawn to the allure of the untamed wilderness. Little did they know that their journey would take an ominous turn.

As they ventured deeper into the trail, the sunset casting an ethereal glow upon the surroundings, they heard a distant cry—a voice calling for help. Their hearts filled with concern, they followed the sound, their footsteps quickening in a desperate bid to assist the unseen traveler.

Unbeknownst to them, the skin walkers had carefully orchestrated their ruse. They led the unsuspecting group further into the forest, the cries for help growing louder, and the sense of urgency intensifying.

But as the group neared the source of the distress calls, a sense of unease washed over them. Shadows danced among the trees, and a cold breeze rustled the leaves, whispering warnings through the air. Instinct told them that something was amiss.

Sarah, the observant of the group, noticed peculiarities in the behavior of their supposed fellow hiker. The figure moved with an unnatural grace, and its eyes gleamed with an unsettling intensity.

Gathering their wits, Amy, Jack, and Sarah realized the true nature of the situation—they were in the presence of the skin walkers. Fear clenched their hearts, but determination fueled their actions. They knew they had to escape the clutches of these malevolent beings.

In a moment of courage, Amy took the lead, guiding her friends away from the false cries and back toward the safety of the main trail. Their hearts pounded in their chests as they sprinted through the forest, the skin walkers pursuing them with an eerie persistence.

As the first rays of sunlight began to pierce through the canopy, the skin walkers retreated, their power diminishing with the rising sun. With each step, the group felt a glimmer of hope and the promise of escape from this harrowing encounter.

Finally, they burst out of the forest, their breaths ragged and their bodies trembling. They had survived the clutches of the skin walkers, forever marked by the encounter.

From that day forward, Amy, Jack, and Sarah warned others of the dangers that lurked in the secluded hiking trail, cautioning them to be vigilant and to heed the signs of deception. The legend of the skin walkers lived on, a reminder that darkness could exist even in the beauty of nature.

And so, in the mountains of Sacramento County, where the legend of the skin walkers whispered through the rustling leaves, hikers walked with an extra measure of caution, their senses heightened and their steps accompanied by the knowledge that danger could lurk in the most unexpected places.

Lakeside Park's Secret

In the heart of Sacramento County, there existed a seemingly ordinary public park known as Lakeside Park. Families would gather there on sunny weekends, children would run and play on the grassy fields, and the sparkling lake would reflect the golden rays of the sun. But beneath the tranquil surface of Lakeside Park, a forgotten city lay hidden, its secrets waiting to be discovered.

Legend spoke of an ancient civilization that once thrived in the depths beneath the park—a city rich in history and mystique. Its existence was unknown to most, except for a select few who had stumbled upon its hidden entrance.

One such individual was Ethan, a curious and adventurous young man with a penchant for exploration. He had always been drawn to the mysteries of the world, seeking hidden treasures and forgotten tales.

One summer day, as Ethan strolled through Lakeside Park, a strange sensation washed over him—a whisper in the wind, a gentle pull toward the lake's edge. Intrigued, he followed his instincts, guiding him to a hidden nook beneath a willow tree. There, he discovered a small, moss-covered door—a portal to another world.

Without hesitation, Ethan stepped through the doorway, descending into the depths below. The air turned cool, and the sounds of the park above faded into silence. He found himself in a vast underground city, its grandeur hidden from the world for centuries.

The forgotten city was a marvel of architecture and ingenuity. Magnificent structures lined the streets, adorned with intricate carvings and vibrant murals that told stories of a bygone era. The air was alive with a sense of history and wonder.

As Ethan explored the forgotten city, he discovered that it was once a thriving metropolis—a center of knowledge, arts, and culture. Its inhabitants had flourished, their lives intertwined with the wisdom of ancient times.

Yet, over the years, the city had been gradually swallowed by the passage of time. Its once-bustling streets now echoed with an eerie silence, and its vibrant colors had faded, yielding to the relentless march of years.

Ethan's footsteps echoed through the empty city as he wandered the abandoned alleyways and squares. He marveled at the remnants of a forgotten civilization, his heart filled with a bittersweet mix of awe and melancholy.

The legend of Lakeside Park and the hidden city beneath its surface began to spread. As whispers traveled through the county, more adventurers embarked on their own quests to uncover the secrets buried within the forgotten city.

Together, they worked tirelessly to preserve the memory of the lost civilization, documenting their discoveries and sharing stories of the ancient world that lay beneath Lakeside Park.

 The Book of Legends

In time, the forgotten city became a beacon of history and enlightenment. Archaeologists, historians, and enthusiasts flocked to Lakeside Park, eager to learn from the remnants of a civilization long past.

And so, in the heart of Sacramento County, where the legend of Lakeside Park whispered through the rustling leaves, visitors and locals alike walked with a renewed sense of wonder. They reveled in the beauty of the park above, knowing that beneath its surface, a hidden treasure of history and culture awaited, reminding them that even in the most unassuming places, extraordinary stories could be found.

The Legend of "The Baby's Cry"

In the outskirts of Kansas City, hidden among overgrown fields and crumbling structures, there lay an abandoned village steeped in a chilling legend—the legend of "The Baby's Cry." Whispers of a creature, shrouded in darkness, echoed through the forgotten streets, its eerie cry mimicking that of an innocent child, luring unsuspecting souls to their untimely demise.

Many years ago, the village thrived—a close-knit community filled with laughter and life. But as the years passed, tragedy befell the villagers, and they were forced to abandon their homes, leaving the village to decay in solitude.

It was said that within the desolate remnants of the village, a creature took residence—an entity of malevolence and deception. With each dusk, as the sun dipped below the horizon, the creature awakened, its cries echoing through the empty streets, reaching far beyond the confines of the village.

The legend spoke of unsuspecting travelers who, drawn by the plaintive cries, ventured into the abandoned village, unaware of the peril that awaited them. They would follow the sound, their hearts heavy with concern, driven by an instinct to offer aid to the defenseless child.

As they traversed the dilapidated pathways, shadows danced along the walls, whispering secrets of the village's tragic past. Their footsteps echoed in the silence, their hearts pounding with a mix of compassion and unease. And then, just as they thought they were nearing the source of the cries, a darkness would engulf them, extinguishing their hopes and sealing their fate.

But the legend also spoke of a brave soul—a traveler named Emily—who had heard the tales of The Baby's Cry but remained undeterred. With a heart fueled by determination and compassion, she set out to uncover the truth that lay hidden within the abandoned village.

As Emily approached the outskirts of the village, she could hear the faint cries, carried on the wind like a haunting melody. She steeled herself, aware of the dangers that awaited her. With each step, the cries grew louder, yet she resisted their alluring pull, guided by an inner resolve.

Emily explored the decaying homes and cracked streets, her senses heightened, and her instincts sharp. She sought to understand the nature of the creature, to unveil the truth that lay shrouded in the darkness.

And then, as Emily reached the heart of the village, she beheld the creature—an ethereal figure, both beautiful and terrifying. Its form shifted, blending with the shadows, its eyes gleaming with an ancient knowledge.

But Emily refused to succumb to fear. She approached the creature, her voice steady and resolute. She pleaded with it, imploring it to release the grip it held on the lost souls who had fallen victim to its deceptive cries.

In a moment of revelation, the creature's eyes softened, as if touched by Emily's sincerity. It had long yearned for redemption, trapped in a cycle of tragedy and anguish. It had become a vessel of darkness, its cries born out of a deep-rooted longing for companionship and solace.

With Emily's words of compassion, the creature's facade began to fade, revealing a vulnerable soul yearning for release from its eternal torment. As the first rays of dawn kissed the sky, the creature's form dissipated, its presence no longer a threat to those who dared enter the abandoned village.

From that day forward, the legend of The Baby's Cry transformed—a tale of redemption and forgiveness, reminding all who heard it of the power of empathy and understanding.

And so, in the outskirts of Kansas City, where the legend of The Baby's Cry whispered through the wind, people walked with a newfound reverence for the abandoned village. They carried the memory of Emily's compassion and the creature's release, forever changed by the realization that even in the darkest corners, redemption and light could be found.

Whispers from the Legends

Little truths and sparks that lit the stories...

The Tale of the Sphnex

Did you know? The Sphnex was imagined during a moment of stillness—when strength felt like silence, not sound.

The Feather of the Stellar Phoenix

This story came from a dream where a single golden feather floated through space like it had somewhere to be.

The Forest of Secrets

Inspired by the idea that maybe the forest isn't just alive... maybe it's listening, deciding who's worth trusting.

The Legacy of the Seas

A reflection on how even the most beautiful places—like ships, memories, or people—can sink if they hold too much.

The Baby Sitters from Mars

Born while watching Dhir build a tower out of LEGO and protect it like a tiny god. That spark became a galaxy.

The Devil's Playground

Started as a question: what happens when the cursed want forgiveness more than revenge?

The Moon Frogs

Yes, I know frogs on the moon don't make sense—but legends aren't supposed to be logical. They're supposed to be *felt*.

The Fireflies That Lit the Stars

This one belongs to Dhir. He chased fireflies like they were carrying wishes, and for a second, I believed they were.

The Last Storyteller

Written for those who think their stories don't matter. They do. Especially the ones you tell only once.

The Girl Who Dreamed in Color

A quiet tribute to anyone who's ever been told to stay inside the lines—and gently refused